Kristy and the Copycat

**Other books by
Ann M. Martin**

Rachel Parker, Kindergarten Show-off

Eleven Kids, One Summer

Ma and Pa Dracula

Yours Turly, Shirley

Ten Kids, No Pets

Slam Book

Just a Summer Romance

Missing Since Monday

With You and Without You

Me and Katie (the Pest)

Stage Fright

Inside Out

Bummer Summer

BABY-SITTERS LITTLE SISTER series
THE BABY-SITTERS CLUB mysteries
THE BABY-SITTERS CLUB series
(see back of book for a more complete listing)

Kristy and the Copycat
Ann M. Martin

AN
APPLE
PAPERBACK

SCHOLASTIC INC.
New York Toronto London Auckland Sydney

ISBN 0-590-47012-4

12 11 10 9 8 7 6 5 4 3 2 1   4 5 6 7 8 9/9

Printed in the U.S.A.   40

First Scholastic printing, April 1994

*The author gratefully acknowledges
Nola Thacker
for her help in
preparing this manuscript.*

Kristy and the Copycat

CHAPTER 1

How is a school bus like a person with the flu? Well, they both groan, lurch, cough, wheeze, and heave.

Gross, right? But if you've ever really thought about it, it's true. I mean, if you've ever spent any time on a school bus.

I have — many, *many* mornings *and* afternoons, going to and from Stoneybrook Middle School. I like SMS, don't get me wrong and riding the bus can be, well, interesting. But all the same, that old bus has a lot in common with the symptoms of the flu.

Still, when I'm riding the SMS bus, I can sometimes get some important thinking done. That might sound kind of weird, I know. I mean, school buses, especially *after* school, are going to be right on the edge of absolute chaos, right? But it takes a *lot* of chaos to equal the level of activity at my house when it gets going. What's one school bus full of kids compared to a house with two parents, one grand-mother, five full-time resident kids, two weekend-and-holiday kids, a dog, a cat, two goldfish and a resident ghost?

Not that I'm complaining! I wouldn't have it any other way. But it does make the bus seem sort of peaceful sometimes.

I guess I'd better introduce myself. I'm Kristy. Kristy Thomas. I live in Stoneybrook, Connecticut, where I'm in the eighth grade at SMS. My mother and father were divorced when I was about eight and my father sort of disappeared from our lives, although we get occasional random cards and phone calls from him in California, where he lives now.

So that left my mom, my older brother Charlie, who's four years older than me, my other older brother Sam, who's two years older, me, and my little brother David Michael, who was just a baby. (He's seven now.) We lived next door to my best friend Mary Anne Spier and across the street from another good friend, Claudia Kishi (more about them later).

Then, not too long ago, my mom met Watson Brewer and they fell in love and got married. Pretty amazing. Even more amazing was moving to Watson's house — only it's not a house, it's a mansion, because Watson is a real, live millionaire. Which means that we went from living in a small house (David Michael's room wasn't much bigger than a closet) to a house where we all have our own rooms (which are definitely *not* closets). We also went up a couple of sizes as a family, from my brothers and mom and me to us and Watson *and* Karen Brewer, Andrew Brewer, Emily Michelle, Nannie, and the ghost of Ben Brewer.

Andrew and Karen are Watson's two children from his first marriage. Karen, who's seven, has a world-class imagination, and Andrew, who's four, can be world-class shy. They spend every other weekend and a lot of holidays with us.

Emily Michelle is our newest family member. We adopted her. She's Vietnamese. She's two and a half and *so* cute. She's just learning to talk, something she's not overly enthusiastic about. But she manages to make herself understood, with or without words, that's for sure!

That's where Nannie comes in. She's our maternal grandmother, and when Emily Michelle arrived, Nannie agreed to come live with us to help look after Emily Michelle and all the rest of us. Nannie drives a pink car we call the Pink Clinker (you can sort of tell how it works by its name — a near relative of the school bus, maybe), is a member of a bowling league and, like Watson, an avid gardener.

Needless to say, we all think she is pretty cool.

Shannon and Boo-Boo are the quadrupeds. (Vocabulary words *do* come in handy sometimes. Quadruped means four-legged.) Shannon is a Bernese mountain dog puppy we got a little while after our wonderful old collie, Louie, died. We miss Louie still, but Shannon is very much a member of the family — with a dog imagination to equal Karen's human one, a little stubbornness like Emily Michelle, and enough puppy energy to keep us all busy.

Boo-Boo, on the other hand, does *not*, I think, have any family traits. Boo-Boo is a big, fat, *mean* old gray cat with yellow eyes. He has a short temper and will bite and scratch if provoked. What constitutes provocation is a mystery to all of us. Sometimes just walking by him is enough to earn you a swat on the ankle!

Have I forgotten anybody?

Oh, yeah, the goldfish, and Ben Brewer, the ghost of Watson's great-great-grandfather. Okay, okay, maybe a ghost really doesn't live on the third floor. But Karen (who else?) believes it, and she can be pretty convincing. Ben really does have his own room, too, a bedroom with all his old stuff in it including his rocking chair. And sometimes, Karen has even me believing that Ben Brewer's chair is still rocking, a little, when we visit his room.

So that's our household. It's never, ever dull, and if it sounds chaotic, well, mostly I love it. And who knows? Maybe it's one of the reasons I am so assertive and organized.

And maybe it's my unique organizational skills and training that enable me to use my time on the bus efficiently — like thinking about the Baby-sitters Club (I'm the president, and more about that later, too) and about the Krushers, the, well, unique softball team that I coach.

Which is what I was thinking about when the bus pulled up to my stop. Not the Baby-sitters Club, but about the Krushers. I'd called a Krushers practice for that afternoon and I was trying to think of something to put a new spin on the usual drills. We didn't have any really big games coming up, but the last few sessions had felt sort of blah, although I couldn't put my finger on why. Not the weather — it had been perfect. And not the team — every member who had been at practice had given it his or her all.

But all the same, something had been lacking.

I still hadn't figured out what the problem was or come up with any incredibly brilliant ideas for making the practices more exciting as I hopped off the bus and headed for my house. Maybe something would come to me while I was getting changed into my softball gear.

"Hey, I'm home!" I called, bombing up the front walk. Nannie and Emily Michelle were surveying a flower bed. Emily Michelle was clutching a handful of wilted green plants and dandelions.

"We've been weeding," explained Nannie.

"Super," I said. "Hi, Emily Michelle."

Emily Michelle looked at me unblinkingly. Then she sniffed the dandelions and sneezed.

"Gesundheit!" I said as the dandelions sort of exploded. Emily looked completely shocked for a moment and then she started to laugh. I couldn't help but laugh, too.

"Dandy!" I said and Nannie rolled her eyes at the bad joke as I flung open the door and raced to my room. I was really going to have to hustle to get to practice early (as the coach, I feel like I should, plus it sets a good example).

"Are you ready?" said David Michael, popping out of his room like a jack-in-the-box. He was, baseball cap and all.

"Whoa, David Michael! What are you doing home before me?"

"We got out early," he said smugly. "*Are* you ready?"

"Not quite yet. Give me five, okay?"

Exactly five minutes later, David Michael knocked on my door. I snatched up my baseball cap (it has a picture of a collie on it — I wear it in memory of Louie) and opened the door.

David Michael said, "Oh, good."

I followed him downstairs and back out the front door.

Nannie and Emily Michelle were blowing on the dandelions now, sending tufts of dandelion fur into the air and laughing with each puff.

I waved again and trotted to keep up with David Michael. It looked like *he* was setting an example for the coach.

"A great day for practice," I said later as we rounded a corner and crossed the road to SES. It was, too. The sun was bright and golden, not the thin, pale sun of winter. A breeze was blowing, so it was just a little on the cool side of warm, perfect for any kind of sport. The SES field was that shiny new no-more-winter green that makes you think of baseball and flowers and well, you know, spring.

"Yeah," said David Michael. "Can I unload the equipment bag?"

"You may," I said, hoisting the bag off my shoulder. It wasn't fancy: extra baseballs, a couple of extra bats and gloves, a batting hel-

met, a catchers mask and chest protector —
and a first aid kit! A good coach, like a good
baby-sitter, is always prepared.

And with the variety of kids on the Krushers
team — twenty, with an average age of 5.8,
and a *wide* range of skills — it is extra-
important to be prepared.

Which brought me back to the problem I'd
been turning over in my head while I was
riding the bus.

The Krusher practice blahs.

However, if that is how I felt, clearly the
members of the Krushers did not. Almost
everyone showed up on time. My friend Claudia Kishi arrived with four-year-old Alicia Gi-
anelli; Mary Anne showed up with the Arnold
twins, Carolyn and Marilyn; and Logan Bruno
(he's an alternate member of the BSC) arrived
with Mathew and Johnny Hobart — all BSC
jobs.

"Want some help?" called Claudia.

I shook my head. "No, thanks. But all cheering is welcome."

"You got it." Claudia settled back on one of
the benches with Alicia on her lap and began
rooting around in her backpack. I was guess-
ing that she had some junk food stashed inside
(Claudia is a junk food *gourmet*) but I was
wrong. She pulled out a pair of sunglasses:
the frames were plain round wire rims, but

the green plastic lenses were square, stuck into the frames by their four corners. I had to smile. Claudia definitely has style, and it's definitely, uniquely hers.

Mary Anne grinned, too, and settled in beside Claudia with the twins on one side and Logan Bruno, who is Mary Anne's boyfriend (more about *all* of this, I promise, in a little while) on the other. Mathew and Johnny settled in beside Logan, and began watching everything intently.

By now all the Krushers had arrived.

I pulled the bill of my hat down and shouted in a good umpire-coach voice: "Okay, let's *play ball!*"

We started with fielding grounders. Right away, a ball skipped up and hit the bill of Jackie Rodowsky's hat, flipping it off and nearly giving me a heart attack. Jackie didn't seem to notice. The BSC calls Jackie "the Walking Disaster" because although he's a cool kid, he *does* manage to get into all kinds of scrapes. Of course, he's used to it, so he's never as upset as the people around him are. "I stopped it, Kristy!" he shouted reassuringly now, snagging both the ball and his hat.

I took a deep breath and said as calmly as I could, "Good work, Jackie!" A Jackie Rodowsky disaster was not the kind of practice excitement I had in mind! Fortunately, trouble seemed to steer clear of Jackie after that.

When we'd finished working on fielding, we practiced base running and making throws to the different bases. For that, we did have to get out the first aid kit, but not for Jackie. Karen, who takes her softball very seriously, decided to slide into home plate. Only she slid in headfirst and skinned both her palms.

By the time Karen got up, Mary Anne was already pulling out the first aid kit. I examined Karen's hands, then led her over to Mary Anne.

"The doctor is in," said Mary Anne, holding up a tube of antiseptic ointment and some Band-aids. "Nice slide, Karen."

"Yes," said Karen. "If I decide to be a famous baseball player, I'll need to be able to sliiiide. Like in real games."

"Oh." I could hear the smile in Mary Anne's voice as I started practice back up. A few minutes later, Karen came trotting back onto the field, undaunted.

Claudia, Logan, and Mary Anne and all their baby-sitting charges cheered from the benches. Karen turned and tipped her hat just as she'd seen the players in the major leagues do. Then she continued, stopping in front of me and saying, "What now, coach?"

"Umm, right field," I said. Things didn't

often get hit to right field and I wanted to take it easy on Karen's hands.

"Okay, coach." Karen nodded and went briskly off to right field.

It was a good practice, despite the Jackie Rodowsky near-mishap and the hand slide. When we gathered for a post-practice cheer, everyone looked tired and happy as they shouted, "YEAH, KRUSHERS!"

"You're a good coach," said Claudia as the team dispersed.

"Thanks," I said. But something in my voice must not have sounded too happy.

"What's wrong?" asked Mary Anne. I looked at her, surprised at how easily she'd picked up on my down mood. I shouldn't have been. Not only has Mary Anne known me practically my whole life and not only is she my best friend, but she is also a very sensitive, caring person.

"Nothing," I said.

"Nothing?"

"Except, well . . ."

"Well?" prompted Mary Anne.

"Well, I don't know. I'm having the softball blahs, I guess. I mean, coaching is fun, but it's hard for me to keep focused on it right now for some reason."

"The softball blahs," said Logan. "Hmmm.

11

Are we talking pre-season slump?"

"I guess," I said slowly . . . and then suddenly it hit me. "No! That's not it. It's the pre-season softball *coaching* slump."

My mind went back to the feeling I'd had when David Michael and I had walked out onto the playing field earlier that afternoon. Excitement. The thrill of victory. The agony of defeat. Playing the game. *Playing the game.*

"I miss *playing*!" I exclaimed. "That's what it is! I miss *playing* softball!"

"Oh," said Mary Anne. She's not particularly athletic, so I could understand her looking a little puzzled.

But Logan nodded in sympathy. "Yeah, I know what you mean. I could hardly wait to get my cleats on and get back out on the baseball field this year."

Claudia frowned thoughtfully, then said, "Hey, not to worry! I, Claudia, have solved the problem! The SMS girls' softball team tryouts are coming up. I saw a sign at school today. The graphics weren't great but . . ."

"What a great idea, Claud. I could try out for the SMS team!" The idea cheered me up. Skipping over the insignificant detail of tryouts, I instantly imagined myself up at bat, ruthlessly staring down the rival pitcher, ready to knock the cover off the first pitch that had any possibilities in it . . .

Then I remembered. "What about coaching? I can't try out. Playing and coaching at the same time would be impossible!"

"Maybe not," said Mary Anne. "You're a very organized person, remember? If anybody could do it, you could."

"Thanks, Mary Anne. But I've learned my lesson about taking on more than I can handle. Some things can*not* be organized into my schedule. Now, to play softball, I'd have to give something up, like school."

"Give up school? Not a bad idea," said Claudia.

"Yeah, but I don't think they'd let you," said Logan.

I shrugged. "Oh, well. It was a nice idea. But hey, not everybody has their own softball team to coach. Who knows — today the Krushers, tomorrow the major leagues."

Claudia slid her sunglasses down her nose and peered at me over them, striking a movie star pose. "Darling," she drawled, "if anybody can do it, you can!"

We left the field laughing and I didn't mind, too much, the fact that I wouldn't be trying out for the softball team after all.

But I still hadn't figured out a way to cure my coaching slump, either.

CHAPTER 2

I looked at my watch. Five-thirty exactly.

I cleared my throat. "This meeting of the Baby-sitters Club will come to order."

Claudia Kishi ripped open a bag of Gummi Worms, held one up, and dropped it into her mouth.

Mallory Pike pushed up her glasses and said, "You looked like a bird just then, Claudia. You know, one of those baby birds when the mother drops the worm in its mouth."

In the act of opening the record book, Mary Anne Spier stopped and cried, "Ugh! Mal!"

Jessi Ramsey and Shannon Kilbourne started laughing and Claudia lifted up another Gummi Worm and asked, "Is eating worms like eating meat? We'll have to remember to ask Dawn next time we talk to her."

Stacey McGill said, "I don't think *Gummi* Worms count, Claud."

Mary Anne made a hideous face.

14

I cleared my throat again. "Ahem!"

"Sorry, Kristy. Did you want a Gummi Worm?" asked Claudia innocently.

I had to grin. "No thanks," I said.

It was business as usual at one of our meetings of the BSC. I was (as usual) sitting in the director's chair in Claudia Kishi's room, our (usual) meeting place. And (as usual) Claudia had dug out her secret hoard of junk food, this time Gummi Worms and pretzels, for the meeting.

I'm the president of the BSC, Claudia is the vice-president, Mary Anne is the secretary, Stacey McGill is the treasurer, Shannon Kilbourne is the alternate officer (Dawn Schafer is our usual alternate officer, but she is in California right now with her father and brother, so Shannon is taking her place), and Jessi Ramsey and Mallory Pike are our junior officers. Logan is also an associate BSC member who doesn't attend meetings but who takes jobs when none of us can take them.

We're a great group (I'm not bragging, I'm just being honest). We're all different, but our differences work together to bring out the best in each of us — which, of course, helps make us good baby-sitters. In fact, the BSC hardly ever has to advertise anymore. We used to hand out fliers and put them up in supermarkets and stores (sometimes we still do),

15

but now we get most of our business by word of mouth: satisfied customers, parents, *and* kids!

We had no idea we'd be so successful when we got started not all that long ago. I was listening to my mother make phone call after phone call one night trying to line up a sitter for David Michael, and I suddenly had this great idea. What if someone could just make one phone call and reach several baby-sitters?

The baby-sitters I was thinking of were Mary Anne and Claudia Kishi. We were already doing a lot of baby-sitting on our own, so it only seemed logical. But right away we decided that three people weren't enough to run a business. That's when Claudia suggested we ask a new friend of hers, Stacey McGill, who had just moved to Stoneybrook from New York, to join us. Stacey agreed.

We kept getting more and more work. And so not long after that — at Mary Anne's suggestion — we asked Dawn Schafer to join the BSC, too. Dawn had recently come to Stoneybrook from California and she and Mary Anne had become friends.

Then, suddenly, Stacey had to move back to New York. That's when we asked Jessi and Mallory to join us as junior officers. But then Stacey's parents got divorced and Stacey moved back to Stoneybrook with her mother

(her father stayed in New York). And recently, Dawn went out to California for awhile to stay with her brother and her father, so Shannon, who was an associate member, took Dawn's place as alternate officer.

We're very organized. We meet at Claudia's three days a week, Mondays, Wednesdays, and Fridays, from 5:30 until 6:00 (Monday is also BSC dues day). Claudia has her own phone line, so that means our clients can call us then and set up appointments without tying up the phone so other people can't use it.

We also have a record book, which is Mary Anne's responsibility (she's never, ever made a scheduling mistake!) and a notebook, where we each write down what happened at our jobs. That's how we stay up-to-date on our clients: who's teething, new kids who have special requirements, things like that. We're also able to use our different points of view to solve problems — it really helps!

In fact, as I said, having all those sometimes *very* different points of view is what I think makes us so successful.

Take Mary Anne. She's my best friend and two people couldn't be more different. We've known each other practically all our lives. But I've always been part of a large family, while Mary Anne lived alone with her father. Mary Anne's mother died when she was a baby, and Mr. Spier was very, very strict and very, very careful about how he raised Mary Anne. He treated her like a child even when she wasn't (she even wore pigtails until recently!). Then Mary Anne had a talk with her father and he realized she was growing up. Now she wears makeup and no more little-kid clothes (or pigtails). She's even the first one of us to have a steady boyfriend, Logan Bruno. Logan's a Southerner and Mary Anne thinks he looks just like Cam Geary, her favorite movie star.

Mary Anne and I both have brown hair and brown eyes and we're both short (although she's not as short as I am, since I'm the shortest person in our class). As you know, I'm used to speaking up and being in charge, but Mary Anne is shy and sensitive. On the other hand, she may be even more stubborn than I am. She's also very perceptive, but she always sees the best in people.

We wouldn't be living next door to each other anymore even if my mother *hadn't* married Watson. Mary Anne moved, too, when her father remarried — Dawn's mother!

It turned out that Mr. Spier and Mrs. Schafer had both grown up in Stoneybrook and known each other in high school (when Mrs. Schafer was Sharon Porter). Then Sharon Porter moved to California and met Dawn's father and married him and had Dawn and Dawn's younger brother Jeff. But they got divorced. That's when Mrs. Schafer moved back to Stoneybrook with Dawn and Jeff and met Mr. Spier again and remarried. Jeff eventually decided to go back to California to live with his father, and Dawn, who missed them, decided not too long ago to go back and stay with them for awhile.

But Mary Anne and Dawn are still best friends as well as sisters.

I was, I admit, a little jealous when Mary Anne became best friends with Dawn. I didn't want Mary Anne to have two best friends. But when I got to know Dawn, it wasn't so hard and I didn't feel like I had to compete with her for Mary Anne's friendship after all.

Dawn doesn't eat meat (if you haven't guessed from what Claudia said about worms). Or much sugar. Or junk food. She has long, long, pale blonde hair, blue eyes, two holes pierced in each ear, and is tall and thin. She has strong opinions, but she is pretty easygoing and down-to-earth, which makes her love of ghost stories all the more surprising. Also pretty amazing is the fact that the Spier-Schafer family now lives in a spooky, old farmhouse (Dawn says it's haunted). It even has a secret passageway that leads from her room to the barn.

When Dawn left for California, it was hard on all of us, especially Mary Anne. But we understand why she did it. It is hard to be separated from people — and places — that you love. We're hoping she'll come back soon, but meanwhile, she's still a member of the BSC. I guess you could say the BSC has an office in California now.

Like Dawn, Stacey is tall and thin and she watches what she eats. She has to. Stacey is diabetic. Diabetes is a condition in which your pancreas doesn't make enough insulin. That means your blood sugar is out of control and could make you faint or even get sick. Stacey has to really be careful about what she eats *and* she has to give herself a shot of insulin every day. Because of her diabetes, Stacey suffered from overprotective parents, just as Mary Anne did. Stacey had to convince them that she could be responsible and take care of herself. Anyway, that's why at every meeting of the BSC, Claudia always has junk food — and not-so-junk food, like pretzels or crackers or fruit.

Anastasia Elizabeth McGill (that's her real name, but you'd better not call her anything but Stacey!) is a real New Yorker, with a sort of New York look. She's one of the most fashionable dressers in the club, along with Claudia (although Claudia's style is different).

Today, for example, while the rest of us were in the usual sorts of clothes — jeans, sweaters, big shirts — Stacey had pulled her permed blonde hair back with a leopard-print scarf tied under one ear. She was wearing one of her favorite pairs of earrings, gold leaf-shaped ones. She was also wearing a black wrap long-sleeve top, a short, low-slung brown skirt with a big belt, black tights, and leopard print flats. She looked extremely cool. Which of course she is.

She's also extremely good in math, which is why she is the BSC treasurer. In fact she's a good student — not at all like her best friend, Claudia.

What can I say about Claudia? She's as cool as Stacey. But if Stacey's style is New York, Claudia's is — planetary. Out of this world. Planet Claudia.

She's very artistic and creative and she's going to be an artist — she's already won a prize for her work. As you might guess, her eye for color and style shows in the way she dresses. Today she was into big: a big yellow shirt with red X-shaped buttons, enormously baggy white pants, and big red Doc Martens double-laced with black and yellow shoelaces. Her long straight black hair was pulled up on top of her head with more black and yellow shoelaces braided together. Her earrings said "stop" and "go" — "stop" in her left ear and "go" in her right.

She looked — excellent. Claudia's Japanese-American and with her long black hair and perfect skin, she's beautiful. But being beautiful doesn't mean you can wear anything. At least, not unless you're Claudia Kishi.

Claudia's a bit of a mystery to her family, I think. She has an older sister, Janine, who's a real, live genius, with the test scores (and the grades — although Janine is in high school, she's already taking courses at a local college) to prove it. Claudia, on the other hand is sort of an anti-genius when it comes to school. Her spelling, for example, is *very* creative (although the teachers unfortunately don't think so) and she's had to be tutored in some of her subjects. And where Janine reads Big, Serious books, Claud loves Nancy Drew (she keeps those books hidden, too, since her parents sort of equate Nancy Drew with junk food for some weird reason). But Claudia has earned her family's respect for her artistic genius. In fact, I think she's going to be an extremely famous artist someday.

Two other best friends in the BSC are our junior officers Jessi and Mallory. They're junior officers because they are the younger club members who can't sit at night yet (except for their own brothers and sisters). They're in sixth grade and the rest of us are in eighth grade. We even used to baby-sit for Mal and the other Pike kids (Mal has four younger brothers — three of them are identical triplets — and three younger sisters) before she joined the BSC. Having all those siblings gave Mal a lot of baby-sitting experience and made her a natural for the BSC. In addition to being a BSC junior officer, Mal is also secretary of the sixth-grade class.

Mal has pale skin (still a little paler than usual — she came down with mono and was out sick for a whole month and only recently could she go back to school and start baby-sitting again), reddish-brown hair, and she wears glasses and braces. She likes to write and draw and would like to be a children's book writer and illustrator someday.

It's not surprising Mal and Jessi are best friends. They have a lot in common. They both *love* horses and horse stories, they're both the oldest in their families, and they both have pet hamsters.

But Jessi's not into writing or drawing, she's into dance. She wants to be a professional ballerina and she's already studying and working hard toward her goal. She takes special dance classes after school in Stamford and she has danced in some big stage performances.

Jessi's family is a little smaller than Mal's —

she's got a younger sister, Becca, who is eight and a half, and the cutest baby brother, John Philip, Jr., whom everyone calls Squirt. There's also her mother, father, and her aunt Cecelia (like Nannie, she moved in to help out).

Jessi has brown eyes, brown skin, and carries herself like a dancer, very graceful and upright.

Shannon Kilbourne is the only BSC member who goes to a private school. She lives across the street from me with her mother and father and her two sisters, Tiffany and Maria. When I first moved into Watson's I thought the whole neighborhood was pretty snobby and Shannon was the worst. Now we laugh about the misunderstandings and tricks we pulled on each other, and I can't believe all that ever happened.

Another important member of Shannon's household is Astrid. Astrid is a Bernese mountain dog and she's especially important because she is the mother of our Bernese mountain puppy, Shannon (who is named after Shannon). Shannon gave the puppy to us when our old collie Louie died. We still miss Louie, but Shannon (the puppy) is a great dog. So is Shannon. (A great person, I mean.)

So that's the BSC.

I looked around the room and thought, as

24

usual, what a terrific club we were, and then the phone rang.

I picked it up. "Baby-sitters Club," I said.

"Kristy, this is Mrs. Engle."

"Oh, hello," I said. "What can we do for you?"

I heard the smile in her voice as she answered. "Karen and Andrew need a baby-sitter this Saturday afternoon."

"This Saturday afternoon? I'll check our schedule and call you back."

Mary Anne already had the appointment book open when I hung up the phone.

"Jessi, it's you, me, or Mal," she said.

"You'll have to count us out," said Jessi. "Mal and I are working on a science project that afternoon."

"The behavior and care of horses?" teased Shannon.

Mal shook her head regretfully. "No. The teacher assigned 'Light and the Color Spectrum.' "

"Speaking of projects, Karen's got one of her own right now," I said. "She's going through a phase, I guess: she really, really wants to be thirteen instead of seven."

"Tell her being a grownup is *tough*," said Claudia.

"Yeah," said Mal. "Look at our science project!"

We all laughed and Mary Anne said, "Okay, I'll take it, then." She carefully wrote her name in the book as I picked up the phone to call Karen's mother back.

We had practically a record-breaking afternoon, so many jobs that we had to call up Logan and schedule him for two of them. I was actually glad when the phone stopped ringing at five minutes to six.

"Whew," said Stacey, echoing my thoughts.

"Yeah," I said.

Claudia passed the Gummi Worms and pretzels around again. "We need to build our strength back up," she told us solemnly. "It's carbo-loading. Like athletes do, you know."

"Speaking of athletes," I said. "I keep thinking about the SMS tryouts for the softball team."

"I think you should go for it, Kristy," said Claudia.

"I don't see how I could. I've been thinking and thinking about it, and I just can't play softball on the team, baby-sit, keep up with my homework, *and* coach the Krushers."

"You couldn't organize your schedule to make it work?" asked Jessi.

"Remember when I ran for class president?" I asked.

"And dropped out because it was too much, even for the world's most organized person,"

26

said Stacey. "We remember. You did the right thing."

"Well, if I couldn't add being class president to my schedule, I couldn't add softball. Not without dropping something else."

"Drop homework!" suggested Claudia and we all laughed.

"I wish I could. But the only thing I could really drop would be the Krushers. And I'd hate to. I mean, I don't think I *could* let them down that way."

"You wouldn't have to drop them," said Stacey. "Let someone else coach them during your softball season. Then you can come back and take over."

"But who? Who would coach the Krushers?" I asked.

The room was silent for a minute. Then Stacey and Claudia looked at each other and said, together, "We would!"

I almost laughed. But I caught myself just in time. I also didn't open my big mouth and say what I was thinking, which was, "You're *kidding*."

Because after a moment I realized that they weren't. *Stacey* and *Claudia* had just volunteered to take over coaching the Krushers!

I tried to imagine what that would be like, and failed. I mean, I knew that Stacey and Claudia knew something about softball from coming to the Krusher practices with baby-sitting charges and from cheering us on at our games. But it was hard to reconcile the image of the two most fashionable girls at SMS with the image of a Krusher softball practice: running bases, fielding balls, pitching, talking strategy.

Realizing that if I let the silence go on any longer, it would be rude, I swallowed and said weakly, "Well, I don't know. It's a lot of work."

Fortunately, Jessi came to my rescue. "Why don't you just try out for the softball team, Kristy. See if you make it. Then decide what to do."

"Well," I said again. Then, "Okay. That's it. That's what I'll do. If I make the team, we'll go from there."

"You'll make it," said Claudia confidently. "And we'll be the new Krusher co-coaches! Right, Stace?"

"Right," said Stacey. "And not only will the Krushers be the best kids' softball team in Stoneybrook. But they'll have a whole new style to go with it!"

CHAPTER 3

"Eeeuw," said Stacey. "What are you doing?"

I looked down at my lunch tray. I had blueberry pie, two helpings of macaroni and cheese, and two rolls.

"What do you mean, what am I doing?"

Stacey sat down across from me and said, "Well, I don't think that's what *anyone* would call a balanced meal. What happened to vegetables? Or, for that matter, fruit?"

"I'm carbo-loading," I said. "These are all high-carbohydrate foods."

"It's true," said Claudia unexpectedly. "You know, the night before the Boston Marathon, they always serve a traditional pasta dinner."

"And for your information, the pie counts as fruit," I said. I studied my plate for a moment and added, "You know, you could also think of macaroni and cheese as worms.

Worms are probably very high in protein . . ."

"Ugh!" That was Mary Anne.

"Dead worms," I said, digging in.

"Kristy!" wailed Mary Anne, turning a little green.

"Okay, okay," I said. "Sorry. It's only macaroni. I think. This *is* the SMS cafeteria, after all."

We — Mary Anne, Stacey, Claudia, Logan and I — were having lunch in the SMS cafeteria. And the SMS cafeteria often serves that universal lunchroom gourmet item, mystery meat. But although the mystery meat doesn't bother me, I was avoiding it today. I really was (sort of) trying to carbo-load, for the SMS softball tryouts that afternoon.

"So, does anybody know anything about the SMS softball team, besides the fact that they made it to the regional finals last year?" I asked.

"Coach Wu is one of the toughest coaches at SMS," said Logan. "Maybe in the whole state. She's the one who suggested the speed workouts to our coach." He made a wry face. "They're killer."

"Great," I said. Not enthusiastically. My vision of me at the plate, about to sock a home run out of the park, was fading fast.

"Kristy," said Stacey. "You're tough. You're

pretty fast. And you're a good player. I don't think you have anything to worry about."

"Maybe," I said. (I was worried.)

"If it were easy, and you made the team, it wouldn't mean as much," Mary Anne pointed out.

I thought about that for a moment. "True," I said. I dug into my macaroni worms. No, I didn't want it to be easy. Well, not *too* easy. But I didn't want it to be too hard, either. I decided to eat everything on my plate, down to the last carbo. Because it sounded like I was going to need all the help I could get.

I spent the rest of the day worrying about tryouts and checking on my trusty softball glove, which was in my regular locker. I'd left all my other gear in my gym locker, but I kind of wanted to keep my glove nearby, for luck. It made me less nervous.

And I *was* nervous. In spite of my friends' confidence in me, I wasn't all that sure I had a chance to make the team. I didn't know how good everybody else who was trying out was. Knowing the team had made it to the regionals and realizing just how tough Coach Wu was supposed to be didn't help.

On the other hand, I'd also found out that lots of the players had graduated, which meant there would be more positions on the team open. And if Coach Wu was as good as she was tough and *if* I made the team, I could learn a lot.

If.

If, if, if.

I wasn't sure I was ready for this . . .

At last my final class was over. I went back to my locker, got my glove, and headed for the girls' locker room.

I pushed open the locker room door to a blast of noise and motion. Good grief. There were about a million people trying out for the team! Trying not to stare or get psyched out, I went to my gym locker, got out my gear, and started to change.

After a minute or two, I realized that I didn't really know all that many people who were trying out. Those I did know, I didn't know very well. I recognized a couple of girls. One of them, Bea Foster, was another eighth-grader who was in my math class. Like Stacey, Bea seemed to be a math whiz, but unlike Stacey she was neither thin nor blonde nor did she seem as strong-willed. Bea had long black hair she wore in a braid straight down her back and she wasn't much taller than I was. I wondered if she was a good player.

Just as I finished tying my shoes, the door leading from the locker room to the fields slammed open and a brisk voice said, "Everybody out for tryouts!'' A blast of the whistle punctuated the end of the sentence and I jumped.

"Whew!" said someone, putting her hands to her ears.

"Wu. Coach Wu," said a tall, solidly built girl wearing the jersey from last year's SMS softball team. "You can tell by the whistle!"

A wiry red-headed girl said nervously, "Is she — mean?"

The tall girl shrugged and headed for the door without answering.

The red-haired girl pulled up her socks, straightened her shoulders, and followed.

I picked up my glove and punched my hand into the well-grooved pocket a couple of times. Then I joined the rest of the players heading out onto the field.

We started out easy. Coach Wu introduced herself, told us how many players she'd be choosing, what the positions were, and a little bit about the team. "My criteria are teamwork, hard work, and talent, in that order," she announced. "Because if you can't play as a team, if you're not willing to work hard, then all the talent in the world isn't going to make you a winner."

She lifted the whistle she wore on a silver chain around her neck and blasted it again (I could tell I'd better get used to it!) and we all trotted out onto the field to begin stretches and then warm-ups by throwing softballs to each other.

After the warm-ups, Coach Wu put us through some basic drills. I relaxed a little. Most of the drills were familiar variations on the ones I used for the Krushers. I let go of my nervousness and worked hard at doing every drill as perfectly as possible.

As the tryouts went on, I realized that several of the players — among them the tall girl who'd shrugged off the question about Coach Wu in the locker room — were consistently pairing off for the drills, and that they played together and talked together easily. It wasn't long before I also realized that they were team members from the year before.

And that they were good.

Very good.

And that they knew it.

Not that they were show-offs or anything. Show-offs are insecure. They crave attention. These players didn't seem to care if you paid attention to them or not. Nor did they seem to see any reason to pay attention to anyone else. They didn't really try to talk to anyone else.

Maybe teamwork meant only talking to people on your own team, I thought wryly, watching them.

But they *were* good. When we were doing fielding drills, one of them snagged a fly ball over her shoulder with her bare left hand. It was an amazing catch, and I winced as I heard the ball hit the palm of her hand.

"Hey, Marcia, quit showin' off," drawled the tall girl, who was playing first base.

"Is your hand okay?" called Coach Wu.

Marcia nodded, although even I could see from where I stood at third that her palm was bright red. "No problem," she answered with studied casualness, and sauntered back to her position at shortstop.

Very tough.

Just then, I heard the bat connect with the ball and the next thing I knew a screaming line drive was headed down the third base line toward me. I reacted instinctively, crouching a little and centering my glove. The ball smacked into it, I grabbed it with my left hand, and winged it to first base. The tall girl caught it easily.

"Nice work," said Coach Wu. To me!

The girl on first base tossed the ball in the air and looked across at me. She raised her eyebrows.

I nodded, trying to look casual, pulled the bill of my own cap down lower, and settled back into position.

Nice work, the coach had said. And it had

been, too. But I couldn't let that break my concentration.

The tryouts went on and on and on. By the time I got to take a rest on the bench near the end of tryouts, I was pretty beat. Under Coach Wu's instruction, I'd done softball drills I never even knew existed before. I'd run farther and faster than I thought possible. I tried a new batting stance and half a dozen fielding positions.

Whatever happened, I'd have some new things to show the Krushers.

Marcia and a couple of other girls walked slowly by. I wasn't sure, but I thought Marcia glanced over at me. As they passed, their voices sank. Were they talking about me? I hoped they were saying I was a good player. Coming from one of them, it would mean something.

Instead, I heard the words, " . . . about the initiation for . . ." before someone else said, loudly, "Shhh!"

I frowned. Initiation? Nobody did stuff like that anymore.

Did they?

No. I must have made a mistake. I probably hadn't heard right.

Before I could think about it further, Coach Wu blew her whistle. "Okay. You've all done a good job. I'll post the results Friday afternoon. If you do not make the team, please remember that we have had many, many good players try out this year. Not every good player will make it. If you don't, I hope I'll see you here next year. Now — four laps around the track at a cool-down pace, and I'll see some of you for the first practice next week. Thank you all."

She blasted the whistle again and I got to my feet. Four laps.

I mustered my last bit of energy to mount a respectable cool-down pace. I was tired. But I'd done well.

I only hoped I had done well enough to make the team.

"So how'd it go, slugger?" That was Charlie.

"That's Ms. Slugger to you," I said, pretending to put my nose in the air.

"She got you, Charlie," said Sam.

"Seriously, Kristy, what did happen at tryouts today?" asked Watson.

I looked down at my mashed potatoes. I was so tired and sore I thought I might fall asleep in them, but I was still strangely exhilarated, too.

"It went pretty well, I think." I told my family about the catch at third and Coach Wu's encouraging words. "And I got some solid hits. Nothing spectacular, though."

"Well, the best batters aren't successful at the plate more than three times out of ten," my mother pointed out. "That's why batting averages are always in the two hundreds and three hundreds — it means two or three hits out of every ten times at bat."

"I never thought about it that way." Did I have the strength to lift another forkful of mashed potatoes?

"It's a good team," said Sam. "But if you do make it, you'd better be *ready*."

"Ready for what?"

Sam made his face solemn. "To prove yourself worthy."

"What are you talking about, Sam?"

"Initiation, what else?" said Sam. "Doing something to show you're good enough to join a team, or club, or whatever. But don't be afraid. I don't think they're allowed to drive you out to the country in the middle of the night blindfolded, and then drop you off."

Watson said, "I don't imagine initiations of any sort are practiced these days. I'd be surprised if they were."

Charlie shrugged. "Sam's just kidding. But you always hear stories. Like the girl who had to spend the night in a haunted house."

"No problem," I answered. "Don't forget, Charlie, *we've* spent the night in a haunted mansion!"

"Oh, yeah. Right. Well, what about the girl who had to wear the same clothes to school for a week without washing them?" said Charlie.

"Pee-uuu," said David Michael. "You won't do that, will you Kristy?"

"I don't think so," I said. "I've never heard of anything like this."

"Coach Wu wouldn't allow it," said Charlie. "But what she doesn't know. . . ." He wriggled his eyebrows.

I rolled my eyes back at him. "Very funny," I said. "I may be tired, but I'm not so tired I'm going to fall for any of this!"

I suddenly remembered the words I overheard and my voice trailed off.

"No, but you might fall into the mashed potatoes," my mother said, laughing. "You sound exhausted. Why don't you go on to bed, Kristy?"

"Yeah, slugger, I'll pinch hit with the dishes for you," said Sam.

"Well . . ." I hated to admit how tired I was. But why pass up a chance not to have to do the dishes? "Okay. Thanks, Sam."

"No prob."

I got up slowly from the table and made my achy way to my room. I was almost too tired to think. But still, as I got ready for bed, I couldn't help wondering: if I made the team, would I have to go through some sort of initiation? I'd never heard of anything like that at SMS for any of the sports. But my brothers said they had.

And what about what I'd overheard?

On the other hand, my brothers were *always* teasing me.

They were probably teasing me now.

Or were they?

CHAPTER 4

More than the usual number of days came between the Monday of softball tryouts and Friday, when the results were supposed to be posted. And all of the days were extra long. They really were.

Or at least they seemed that way.

I tried not to talk about it, or let anyone know how focused I was on whether I'd made the team or not. But I admit, I was a little preoccupied during the BSC meetings, and while I kept up with my homework, I wasn't exactly into it.

Friday morning, I thought the bus would *never* get to SMS. It took twice as long. I was amazed to see, as I bounded up the front steps, that the bus had arrived at the usual time.

A crowd of people had gathered around the bulletin board outside the gym. For a moment I stood at the edge, gathering up my courage.

A soft voice at my elbow said, "Go on, Kristy."

I jumped. "Mary Anne! What are you doing down here?"

Mary Anne smiled. "Oh, Kristy. How could I forget that the results of the tryouts were being posted today?"

"Have you looked?" I asked.

"Kristy! Go look for yourself!" Mary Anne gave me a little nudge and I plunged into the crowd.

What a short list, I thought as I got closer. Too short. Too short for me to be on it.

Well, I wasn't going to be disappointed. In fact, I was going to try out again next season and besides . . .

My brain registered what my eyes had been looking at. "I made it!" I gasped. "I made it!"

I wriggled back through the crowd to Mary Anne.

"Congratulations, Kristy," said Mary Anne, before I could even speak.

"*Did* you look at the list before I got here?" I demanded.

Mary Anne nodded. "But even if I hadn't, I'd have been able to tell from your face."

I had to laugh. I was *so* excited. "This is super!" I said.

"It really is, Kristy!" Mary Anne threw her arms around me and gave me a big hug. "Listen, I have to go, but I'll see you at lunch, okay?"

I nodded in a happy daze as Mary Anne hurried off. I had made the team. Suddenly, the whole world looked different.

A league of my own, I thought.

"Congratulations," said another voice and I turned to see Bea.

"Thanks," I said. I paused. I hadn't really noticed who else had made it. I didn't have to wonder long.

"Isn't it great?" Bea shrieked. "I made it, too!"

"Congratulations!"

Bea motioned excitedly to two other girls standing beside her. "We *all* did — Tonya, Dilys, me, and you. *And* we're the only new members on the team!"

That stopped me. "Really?"

"No pressure," murmured the curly-haired girl on Bea's right. "Hi. I'm Tonya. You probably don't know me or Dilys. I'm in seventh grade, and Dilys is . . ."

"A sixth-grader," Dilys said. "Don't rub it in. Not only am I one of the four new members of the team, but I'm the *only* sixth-grader."

"You're so tall. You don't *look* like a sixth-grader," I blurted out. "Ooops. Sorry."

Dilys laughed. "Don't be. It's a compliment. I can hardly wait to not be a sixth-grader anymore, so not looking like one is a good beginning."

We all started laughing, and then Bea and Dilys started talking at top speed. Tonya, like me, was silent. I wondered if she was savoring the feeling of making the team as I was. I caught her eye and smiled.

"So, you're the new girls." I recognized the raspy tone and looked up. Yes. It was Marcia, the girl from the tryouts, flanked by Tallie, the pitcher.

Marcia took a step forward and Bea backed up, bumping into me. I didn't move. What was going on?

"You think because your name was put up on the board with ours that you've got it made? That you're a member of the team?" asked Marcia.

Bea said, "Coach Wu — "

"Forget Coach Wu." That was Tallie. She had a funny little smile on her face. "This isn't about Coach Wu. It's about you. The Four Musketeers here."

"Hey," I said, beginning to feel annoyed, but trying to turn it off. It wouldn't do to get a bad start on the team. "Hey, I like that. Not a bad name."

"Yeah?" asked Tallie, turning to inspect me. In spite of myself, I blushed, feeling like a complete dork.

I raised my chin. "What's the problem, Tallie?"

Tallie kept staring hard at me as she answered, "No problem. It's just this: You're not a member of the team until you pass initiation."

"Initiation!" squeaked Bea.

So Charlie and Sam had been right, I thought. I said aloud, "Initiation? You mean hazing? SMS doesn't allow that."

"Very good," Marcia drawled. "But the SMS softball team *does*."

"I don't know." Dilys shook her head.

"You don't have a choice," Marcia told her. "You don't do your initiation, you don't play, it's as simple as that."

"Wait a minute," I said. "You can't do that! It's up to coach, not you."

"Have you ever played ball with someone who makes you look bad no matter what you do?" said Tallie. "They put a little spin on their throws so you fumble the ball, slide into you at practice, give you the signal to run when you should stay on base?"

"You wouldn't do that!" Tonya said.

"Check it out," said Tallie with a truly evil grin.

No one answered. Then Marcia said, "This is what you're going to do, musketeers. You're going to spray paint grafitti on the equipment shed at the edge of the track."

I made one last try. "Does the rest of the team know about this?"

Marcia stepped forward and glared at me. "Yes. We all decided on the initiation task. What's the matter? Chicken?"

"No, but I'm not stupid, either," I began, when Tallie said, "Marcia," in an urgent undervoice.

Marcia looked past me and broke into a big smile. "So welcome to the team," she said. "Anything we can do, just let us know, you hear?"

"Huh?" said Bea.

"Break it up, girls," Coach Wu said from behind me. "The warning bell has already rung, you know."

"Right, coach," said Tallie. She looked at us. "See you."

"Later," added Marcia meaningfully and they sauntered off down the hall.

"I'm going to be late," gasped Dilys. She shot off down the hall.

"Me, too," said Tonya. " 'Bye."

" 'Bye," cried Bea and hurried after her.

Still seething, I ran toward my own first class and slid into my seat just as the bell rang. Maybe almost being late was why I was so distracted.

Or maybe it was thinking about what Marcia and Tallie had said. Surely they were kidding about the hazing.

Or maybe I was kidding myself.

"It's a pop-up Oreo!" Claudia pitched a cookie up into the air, thumped her fist into her hand, and then caught it.

"OUT!" cried Stacey.

"You guys are too much." All the brooding I'd been doing about the initiation scene that morning went right out of my head as I stepped into Claudia's room. The members of the BSC had beat me there. They'd put up a banner that said, "Kristy at bat! Hooray!" And there was an ice-cream cake on a card table set up right in the middle of the room.

"Okay, Claud," I said, stepping into the room and making an elaborate pretense of looking around. "I know you made a cake for me. Where have you been keeping it?"

When we stopped laughing, Claudia pulled the director's chair up to the table. "You have the honor of cutting the cake."

I divided it up into big chunks for everybody except Stacey, who was eating fruit salad and yogurt.

"Is this the carbo-loading you were telling me about?" asked Mallory.

"Definitely," I said.

"So when Claud and I coach the Krushers, we should keep this victory food in mind?" Stacey motioned at my heaped plate of ice cream cake with her fork.

"Right again."

"Oh, we are going to be *excellent* coaches," said Claudia. "We've just figured out the key secret."

"Well, there's a little more to it than that," I began. But then the phone rang.

"ThismeetingoftheBSCwillcometoorder," I said hastily and picked up the phone.

"So, Kristy, any other tips on coaching the Krushers?" asked Claudia after we'd finished setting up the appointment.

"Uh, yeah," I said.

"Wait a minute," said Stacey. She dug around in her pack and pulled out her notebook.

"What are you doing?" I asked.

"Taking notes."

"Oh."

"Well, go ahead," Stacey urged.

Everyone was looking at me. But how do you coach a coach? Or a pair of coaches? Especially coaches who have never coached before?

Or possibly even played softball.

"Um, well, you've played softball before, right?"

Both Stacey and Claudia looked indignant.

"Of course I have," said Stacey. "You think there aren't any softball fields in New York?"

"Me, too," said Claudia. "I mean, I've played too."

Shannon said softly, "Uh-oh."

"When?" I asked, trying to sound neutral.

"In school," said Stacey. "It was part of phys ed."

"Yeah," said Claudia.

"Right. So you've got the basics."

"Yep." Claudia made a pitching motion with her hand. "A pitch has to go over the plate to be a strike."

"A full count is two strikes and three balls." That was Stacey.

"Well, you're both right," I said, trying to break it to them gently. "But that kind of thing is a little sophisticated for the Krushers. We do real basic stuff. You know, base running drills, drills on plays to first and second, catching fly ball drills."

A long silence followed my words. Stacey and Claudia, and for that matter, Shannon, Jessi, and Mary Anne all looked at me blankly. Only Mallory nodded in comprehension.

"We do stuff like that in our family," Mallory explained. "You know, when you have so many kids, you figure you might as well

49

do some real practicing instead of just throwing the ball around."

The blank looks remained on the others' faces.

"Drills," I said. "You know, doing something over and over again until you get it right."

"I know what a drill is," Claudia finally said. "Homework." She made a face.

"I never thought about it like that, Claud, but I guess you're right."

"I guess this means we won't be practicing double plays and squeeze plays and bunts," said Stacey with a sigh.

"Not at first, maybe." I didn't want to totally discourage her, but as good as the Krushers were, they were not a team that routinely practiced deep baseball (or softball) strategy.

"So, ah, Kristy," Stacey said. "What kind of drills will we practice?"

"Batting practice is good," I said. "You pitch to the team and let them practice batting. That way, you can rotate other players on the field and let them get fielding practice in at different positions.

"Then you can do fielding practice. You stand at the plate and throw the ball up and hit it to different parts of the field and the fielders — in their regular positions — practice fielding. That's where setting up the various

50

plays — things that might happen in a game situation and how to handle it — can also come in — "

"Kristy."

I'd been so intent on explaining a basic practice routine that I'd forgotten who I was talking to. Claudia's voice brought me back to reality.

"Yes, Claudia?"

Claudia pulled out a sketch pad and a pencil and sat down cross-legged on the floor.

"Let's start with batting practice," she said. "Stacey is going to take notes. I am going to draw pictures. Okay?"

"Great idea," I said. "Listen, I'll come to the first practice with you to help out. Don't worry. It'll work out fine. Really."

Stacey suddenly grinned. "You mean that? One coach to another?"

"Coach's honor," I said solemnly. I looked down at Claudia who sat, pencil poised above paper. "Now. About this batting practice. Why don't we start with the layout of the field and the positions, okay?"

"A field is called a diamond . . ."

CHAPTER 5

Saturday

If imitation is the sincerest form of flattery then the thirteen-year-olds of the world should be very flattered by Karen these days. Because she wants more than anything to grow up and be thirteen and the best way to do that is to act like a thirteen-year-old. Or at least, the way Karen *thinks* a thirteen-year-old "grown-up" would act! Did we ever act like that?

"Have a good time, Mrs. Engle, Mr. Engle," Mary Anne said. It was Saturday afternoon and she was baby-sitting for Karen and Andrew while their mother and stepfather went to a garden party. Mary Anne wasn't quite sure what a garden party was, but she thought the Engles looked very garden-y: Mr. Engle was wearing a loose linen jacket and pants and a panama hat, and Mrs. Engle had on a flowered dress with a full skirt and a big hat with a flower pinned to the upturned brim.

"Thank you, Mary Anne. We should be back around six," said Mr. Engle.

Mary Anne and Karen (who uncharacteristically hadn't said a word) waved good-bye. Andrew didn't wave, but he watched until the car had pulled out of the driveway.

That was when Mary Anne expected Karen, the Queen of All Imaginative Games, to want to play a garden party game. And knowing Karen, she was sure it would be *much* more exotic than any real garden party.

But Mary Anne was in for a surprise. Karen didn't want to play any games at all. At least not any of her usual games.

The moment the car disappeared from sight, Andrew yawned. For some reason, that made Mary Anne yawn. And then Karen yawned.

Mary Anne laughed. "I think yawning is

contagious, Andrew, what do you think?"

"I'm not sick!" exclaimed Andrew instantly.

"No, no, of course not. I just meant that when you yawned, it made Karen and me yawn, too."

Andrew thought for a moment, then said, "Oh."

"It's a job for Dr. Sleep," said Karen suddenly.

"Hmmm," said Mary Anne. "What would Dr. Sleep recommend?"

"A nap," said Karen. "Then, dessert."

"Well, Andrew, how does that sound to you?" Mary Anne held out her hand and Andrew put his in it with a sleepy smile. A few minutes later, he was sound asleep in his bed.

"What do you want to do until Andrew wakes up, Karen?" Mary Anne asked as they walked back down the hall from Andrew's room. "Want to play . . ."

But before she could finish Karen said, "How old are you, Mary Anne? Are you thirteen, like Kristy?"

Surprised, Mary Anne answered, "Yes."

"You are? Gigundoly super. No. I mean, that's, that's *excellent*." Karen paused.

"Let's have some lemonade," suggested Mary Anne.

Karen barely nodded, so intent was she on

her own thoughts. Mary Anne soon found out what they were.

"When you're thirteen, can you stay up as late as you want? Do you take neat classes at school? Like biology and dissecting frogs?" (Mary Anne shuddered inwardly.) "Can you dress any way you want? Why aren't your ears pierced like Dawn's are?"

Karen paused to draw a breath and Mary Anne took the opportunity to shove a glass of lemonade in her hand and sit down at the kitchen table across from her.

"Wow, Karen, those are a lot — a gigundoly lot — of questions. Let me see: yes, I can stay up as late as I want, within reason. I usually don't, unless I have a test to study for. If you stay up late, you're tired the next day at school. Yes, we take good classes, but no, I haven't had to dissect a frog yet. I can dress pretty much the way I want to, but nothing wild or extreme. But that's okay, because I think my style suits me just fine. And the reason my ears aren't pierced is because I don't want them pierced."

Now it was Mary Anne's turn to stop for a breath. Karen jumped right in.

"What about sleepover parties? You can stay up as late as you want then, right? How do you decide what clothes you wear? Can you shop *all by yourself*? With your *own* money? How old is old enough to get your ears pierced? Do you have a boyfriend?"

Karen paused and Mary Anne laughed helplessly.

"One question at a time, Karen. I don't know what to answer first."

"Do you have a boyfriend?" Karen repeated promptly.

Mary Anne thought of Logan and smiled. "Yes, I do."

"Wow," breathed Karen. "A real live boyfriend."

"Well, yes," Mary Anne agreed. "A real live boyfriend."

"I have a pretend husband," said Karen. "Ricky Torres. But we had a pretend wedding anyway, so I don't *think* it is the same thing."

"Not exactly," said Mary Anne, keeping her face straight.

"What is your boyfriend's name?"

"You've met him. Logan. Logan Bruno. Would you like some more lemonade?"

Karen shook her head impatiently. "No, thanks. Logan. Hmm."

"I think I'll have a little more." Mary Anne was amused by Karen's questions. But she found Karen's intense scrutiny somewhat un-nerving.

"Maybe I *will* have some," Karen said sud-

56

denly. So Mary Anne poured some lemonade for both Karen and her. She sat back down at the table across from Karen. Karen's blue eyes were enormous behind her glasses.

Mary Anne took a drink of lemonade.

Karen took a drink of lemonade.

Hmm, thought Mary Anne.

"Tell me more about Logan. Is he really that . . ." Karen lowered her voice, "*cute?*"

"I think he is," answered Mary Anne. "I think he looks just like Cam Geary. Only cuter. And he's got this great southern accent. And, let's see. He can be *very* stubborn. But he can be very sweet. Oh, and he's an associate member of the Baby-sitters Club."

"He is?" Karen looked thrilled. "Wow."

"Mary Anne. Mary Annnnnnne." Before Karen could ask any more questions, the sound of Andrew's voice came to them.

"Andrew's awake," said Karen.

"He sure is," said Mary Anne. She finished her lemonade in one gulp, and set the glass down. "Why don't you clear off the lemonade glasses and I'll go get him."

"Okay," said Karen, finishing *her* lemonade in a gulp, too.

On her way out of the kitchen, Mary Anne caught a glimpse of herself in a small mirror above the telephone table. She stopped and smoothed her hair down.

She looked down and realized that Karen was standing behind her and a little to one side, smoothing her hair back in exact imitation of Mary Anne.

Hmmm, thought Mary Anne again.

When she returned with Andrew, Mary Anne suggested that Karen and Andrew might like to play out in the backyard. Both Andrew and Karen agreed immediately. But if Mary Anne thought that Karen was going to put her extremely vivid imagination to work thinking up wonderful games or outrageous charades, she was wrong.

Andrew, still a little slow and cranky from his nap, promptly sat down in the shade of a tree and began excavating holes with an old trowel.

"What are you doing?" asked Mary Anne. "Are you looking for treasure?"

"Worms," said Andrew.

Worms seemed to be a theme this month, thought Mary Anne, shuddering inwardly. Aloud she said, "Oh. What are you going to do with them, Andrew?"

"Dig new homes for them and move them," said Andrew.

"Oh," said Mary Anne. She sat down in an old Adirondack chair nearby and Karen sat down in the one next to her.

"Good grief," said Karen.

Mary Anne looked at her in surprise.

"Worms," Karen continued. "Can you *believe* it?"

"Ah, well," began Mary Anne cautiously. Normally, Karen would have been right down there with Andrew and would probably have tried to persuade Mary Anne to join in too, building worm palaces and making up wild stories of worm wildlife beneath the dirt.

But not this version of Karen.

"What do you think of the weather, Mary Anne?" asked the new "adult" Karen.

"The weather? Oh, it's all right. Ah, how's school?"

"School?" Karen rolled her eyes and crossed her legs at the ankle (Mary Anne had just crossed her legs at the ankle, of course). "Oh, it is so — babyish."

"Babyish," said Mary Anne neutrally.

"You know," said Karen. "I wish we could study something exciting, like you do."

"You have math and art, right? So do we," said Mary Anne.

"It's not the same," said Karen. "Now does Logan have brown eyes or blue eyes or green eyes? What color eyes are your favorite color? What is the first thing you liked about Logan? How could you tell if he liked you? What were you wearing? Something *really* sophisticated?"

"Sophisticated?" Mary Anne repeated, startled.

"You know. Cool."

"I don't remember, exactly. About what I was wearing, I mean."

"I just love boys with green eyes, don't you? Ricky's eyes are not green." Karen shrugged. "My grown-up boyfriend will have green eyes and be very handsome and drive a wonderful car."

"Thirteen-year-olds can't drive."

That stopped Karen, but only temporarily. "Maybe my boyfriend will be a *much older man*. Sixteen. What do you think?"

Remembering Stacey's crush on an "older man" (her teacher) Mary Anne said, "I don't think older men are as much fun. I mean, for boyfriends."

"Really? Well." Karen raised her voice. "Are you having fun, Andrew?"

Andrew looked surprised by the question. "Yes," he said impatiently.

"Oh, good. *Excellent*," said Karen.

Without realizing it, Mary Anne sighed.

Beside her, after the briefest of pauses, Karen sighed too.

Mary Anne had never, ever spent very much time with a copycat. It was like playing a weird game of Simon Says.

And it also was, thought Mary Anne, going to be a long afternoon.

CHAPTER 6

"Hey, you!"

I looked up from where I sat on the bench by the softball diamond, re-knotting my cleats into double knots. Just because I'd made the team didn't mean that I could get slack. What if my shoes came unlaced while I was practicing a big play right in front of Coach Wu?

Tallie and Marcia and another girl, who I remembered as a left-handed player named Coreen, were standing in front of me. "Hey," I said.

Tallie raised her voice. "Tonya, Dilys, Bea, could you come over here? Please."

The way she said please didn't sound like a request, it sounded like a command. It must have sounded that way to the other three new players on the team, because they hustled over, looking a little apprehensive.

"Your initiation is to spray paint the old

shed." That was Tallie, folding her arms and surveying us coolly.

"Soon," added Coreen.

"Very soon," said Marcia.

I looked from one face to the other. They weren't kidding. Marcia and Tallie and Coreen were dead serious.

"No," I said.

"Me, neither," said Dilys. "I mean, no."

Bea and Tonya didn't say anything.

"No?" repeated Tallie. "Why not?"

"Because I don't want to," I said.

"And because it's wrong," said Dilys. "It's vandalism."

Marcia rolled her eyes. "You're kidding! That old shed? A coat of paint, any kind of paint, would improve it!"

I shook my head.

"Listen," said Tallie. "I don't think you understand. This is a *team* initiation, decided on by the *team*. Not doing it means you don't really want to play on our team. Is that what you're saying?"

"No," began Dilys, but before she could go any further, the familiar blast of the whistle sounded from the center of the dugout.

"Okay, girls, let's hustle. Get out there and start warming up!"

Tallie waved her arm and smiled. "Right, coach," she called.

She and Marcia and Coreen trotted away, looking every inch the shining examples of team spirit.

Dilys and Tonya and Bea and I looked at one another.

"Girls?" coach called again. "We haven't got all day. Move it!"

No time to think about it now.

We moved it.

If I'd thought tryouts were tough, I thought Coach Wu's practices were tough to the infinite power. I was so tired after the first one that when I lay down to go to sleep at night, all my muscles kept twitching. And my hand, despite the padding of my trusty softball glove, was tender from catching the balls that had been winged into it. Whatever else I might think about the rest of the team, I had to admire their talent and drive. They could play, really play good ball. In one practice, it seemed, I'd already learned a million new things.

But did they have to throw the ball so hard?

Or was that part of the hazing I'd get if I didn't go along with the initiation?

I turned a little and groaned softly. I had a shiner of a bruise coming up on my knee where a ball had skipped off a rock and creamed me. Huh. They might call them softballs, but when they whacked into your knee at a million miles an hour, there was nothing soft about them.

I'd put ice on it after practice and that had helped.

I'd have to remember to put ice on it tomorrow.

Too bad I couldn't pack my whole aching body in ice. But it would get better, I told myself, gritting my teeth. As I got in shape and got used to being on the team and playing for Coach Wu, things would get better.

And they did.

At least physically.

By the fourth practice, I had learned to absorb the speed of the balls thrown to me in my glove more efficiently, letting my arm give a little, just as the ball went into the pocket, to take the shock. My reactions were getting faster. And I was getting stronger and smarter about how to play softball.

I should have been feeling pretty terrific. Gigundoly super.

But I didn't.

Because Tallie and Marcia and Coreen and all — every single one — of the old team members were making it very clear that they weren't kidding about the initiation plans.

Like Marcia stopping me in the stairwell at school (I felt like I was in some weird scene from *Grease*) and saying, "Well."

"Well, what?" I asked.

"When are you four musketeers going to pass initiation and become real team members?"

"We *are* real team members," I said.

"That's what you think," said Marcia, and walked away.

Tallie and Coreen met Bea and me outside the locker room after practice one afternoon.

"Good workout, huh," said Coreen.

"Killer," said Dilys, and I nodded.

"That's Coach Wu," said Tallie in the friendliest tone of voice I heard her use. "She's killer. But she's fair."

"I like her a lot," I said.

Coreen said, "We don't like to let her down. The team, I mean."

"So what do you think?" Tallie asked. "Is it fair for some members of a team to get special treatment?"

"No," said Dilys slowly.

"I don't think so either," said Tallie. "It kind of ruins team morale. But all of us who have already been initiated kind of think you new guys *are* getting special treatment."

"Because we're not going to participate in hazing?" I said. "That's ridiculous. If Coach Wu knew about this . . ."

Tallie's eyes suddenly blazed with anger. "Coach Wu doesn't know. Nobody knows. We're a *team*. We can keep team things secret — as a team. And to be on this team, you have to do *everything* that's required to be a part of it."

"So what you're saying," said Dilys, "is that if we don't spray paint the shed, we're not part of the team."

"We can make that happen," said Coreen.

She and Tallie left me and Dilys to face one another.

"Oh, Kristy, what are we going to do?" said Dilys, her golden brown eyes miserable.

I felt as miserable as she looked. I shook my head. "I don't know," I answered.

The next practice was a nightmare. Everything that could go wrong, did. No matter how careful I was, I couldn't seem to hold on to the ball. Dilys was having the same problem. We looked like a couple of beginners, dropping balls and flubbing plays.

But Tonya and Bea seemed to be doing just fine. They were fitting right in. And it seemed to me that they were avoiding us.

No one said anything to either Dilys or me after that practice. But then, they didn't need to. They'd made their point. If we didn't go along with what they wanted, they'd make us look so bad Coach Wu would throw us off the team. They'd already intimidated us into playing badly this afternoon.

Nobody said anything to us, and we didn't say anything to each other. Or to anybody else.

At least, I didn't. I didn't know what to say.

I was angry. Angry with them and angry with myself. I hated the pressure they were putting on me. It was wrong. Unfair. But maybe, on the other hand, I was being picky. A big baby. After all, it was only an old shed. Besides, if the other team members had gone through their initiation, maybe it was only fair that we go through ours.

And except for the whole hazing issue, I wanted to be a part of the team. I *loved* playing softball. I loved playing with good players and having my own uniform and all the cool stuff I was learning from Coach Wu and the other players. I loved feeling myself getting in shape, getting better. And better.

I didn't want to quit.

And I sure didn't want to be thrown off the team.

So when Coreen and Tallie and Marcia stopped Dilys and me after the next practice, I took a deep breath and, ignoring the voice inside me that said, "Don't let them push you around," I said to them, "Okay, you've made your point."

I looked at Dilys. Bea and Tonya, I realized, were standing a little to one side, watching. Waiting.

Then I said, "Friday night."

"Dilys?" said Tallie.

Dilys lowered her eyes. Then she shrugged. "What's the big deal, anyway?" she asked. "Why not?"

The forbidding looks that everyone had been wearing melted away.

"Outstanding!" cried Tonya, practically skipping forward. "I'm so glad. Listen, Bea and I have it all planned. We're going to meet at nine o'clock. We're each going to bring a can of spray paint, a different color for each of us. I'm yellow and Bea is green. What about red for you, Kristy?"

Somehow, the idea of color co-ordinating the spray paint was so ridiculous that it almost made me feel better. Almost. At least, it was easier somehow to tell myself that I had let this whole thing get out of perspective. It was all so silly.

"Sure," I said.

"And you'll be blue, Dilys."

Dilys nodded.

"Great," said Bea.

"Congratulations," said Marcia.

Tallie punched Marcia's arm playfully.

"Don't congratulate them yet. Wait till the dreadful deed is done."

As we walked out across the SMS grounds, we passed Coach Wu loading some equipment into her car.

"Good night, coach," called Tallie.

Coach Wu looked up and, seeing us all together, smiled and looked pleased.

"Good night, team," she called.

Needless to say, I spent most of the Friday BSC meeting thinking about the "dreadful deed." I had spent most of Thursday night on the phone with Dilys and Bea and Tonya, making plans. Since I lived so far away from SMS, I'd had to convince Charlie to give me a ride to Bea's house. We were having a softball get together for new members, I told him. At least that was true, more or less. But it wasn't really. It was a lie. The whole evening was a lie.

Like, I wasn't going in Bea's house. I was going to meet Bea and Dilys and Tonya under the tree at the back corner of SMS near the shed.

And then we were going to do our initiation.

"Kristy?"

"Hmm? Oh," I looked up to find the rest of the BSC staring at me.

"Long week, Kristy?" asked Mary Anne.

"Yeah," I said.

Silence.

"Uh, Kristy?" said Shannon.

"Yeah?"

Shannon silently pointed at her watch.

I looked down at mine. Six-oh-five.

"Good grief!" I said. "This meeting of the BSC is officially adjourned!"

"And the week is officially over," said Claudia gleefully.

I didn't say anything. Because it wasn't true for me. The hardest part of my week was just beginning.

CHAPTER 7

I stowed the red spray paint in my backpack and looked at myself in the mirror. I was wearing blue jeans, a dark blue long sleeved shirt, and black hightops. I figured I didn't want to be too visible in the dark, just in case.

Just in case. Just in case what?

We weren't going to get caught, I told myself. I just had to stay calm and get this over with.

I hoisted my backpack and went downstairs and got into the car with Charlie.

"So, how do you like the team?" asked Charlie as we drove toward Bea's.

"It's fun. You won't forget to pick me up at eleven?"

"No. Short party."

"Well, it's been a long week. We're all pretty tired. But we wanted to get together."

"Just the new players, right? Yeah, new players have to stick together, at least at first.

Soon you'll all feel more a part of the team."

If only Charlie knew, I thought. Aloud I said, "Yeah. Well, here's Bea's house. Thanks, Charlie."

Charlie, of course, waited until I got up to Bea's door. I pretended to ring the doorbell, then turned and waved. Charlie waved back and drove off.

I walked quickly (and quietly) down Bea's front walk, then broke into a jog. A few minutes later, I reached the meeting place.

At first, I didn't see anyone. I stopped, my heart pounding. Had they changed their minds?

Then something moved.

"Uh!" I croaked, in spite of myself.

"Chill," said Tonya. "It's me."

"Tonya."

"Yeah. You're the last one. Thought for a minute you weren't going to show up."

"Well, I did." My eyes were getting used to the dark, and I could dimly see Dilys and Bea nearby.

Bea said, "Here."

I felt something small and chalky and faintly warm in my hand. "What is it?"

"Burnt cork," said Bea. She giggled. "I saw it in a movie. You rub it on your face so your skin doesn't stand out so much in the dark."

"Oh." I took the cork and made a few half-hearted swipes at my face. Then I said, "Well, let's get this over with."

"Oh, Kristy. This is *exciting*," breathed Tonya.

I didn't say anything, but I let her lead the way through the dark toward the old shed. We could barely see the outline of it in the faint light reaching us from the entry lights around the doors of SMS.

"De-de, de-de," hummed Dilys. I recognized the opening notes of the old television show *The Twilight Zone*. I couldn't help it. I gave a snort of laughter.

"Shhhh," said Bea, but I could tell that she was barely suppressing laughter, too.

And then we were there. "The target has been reached," I intoned solemnly.

"Women, get out your weapons," added Bea.

We fumbled for a moment, then I heard the sound of the spray paint cans being shaken up.

"Let's each take a side," suggested Tonya.

We split up and I heard Tonya call softly, "On the count of three. One. Two. THREE."

We all began to spray. It was a weird, wild, spooky feeling, spraying at the dim outline of the old shed in the near pitch dark. I didn't try to spray paint anything in particular, just big (nervous) loops and whirls.

At first it was scary. Then after awhile it got monotonous. I was glad we were outside, too. The paint stunk and made my eyes water. But my night vision was getting better and better. It wasn't that hard to see now at all.

I finally stopped. "Whew," I said. "I can't take this anymore!" I staggered back around the shed and joined Dilys, who'd just stopped spraying, too. A few moments later, Tonya and Bea joined us.

"Let's get out of here," I said.

"Yeah," said Dilys.

"Wait," gasped Tonya. She sagged to the ground near the shed and began rooting around in her sling bag and Bea dropped down beside her.

"Mission accomplished!" Bea giggled and reached in her pocket. I suddenly realized that both Bea and Tonya were taking out cigarettes.

"Come on," said Tonya. "Have a cigarette to celebrate."

"No way," I said.

"No *thanks*," said Dilys emphatically at the same time.

"Suit yourself," said Tonya. "I tell you what, I *need* a cigarette. My nerves!"

I wondered who Tonya was copying as she struck the match. It went out. The second one stayed lit, but went out when she raised it to light her cigarette. She finally got it lit and took a big drag — and coughed loudly.

"Shhh!" I said.

Bea, meanwhile, struck one, two, three, four matches in a row, throwing them impatiently to the ground until at last she got her own cigarette lit. She wasn't any more experienced at smoking than Tonya. In fact, she coughed even more loudly.

"Athletes don't smoke," I said. "In fact, people with any intelligence don't."

In answer, Tonya took a long drag on her cigarette and inexpertly blew the smoke in the air.

"I'm leaving," I said. "NOW."

I turned and marched away through the darkness with Dilys beside me. A few minutes later, panting and smelling of cigarettes, Bea and Tonya caught up.

We walked silently back to Bea's house. Bea waited on the porch with me until Charlie arrived and waved as I got back in the car. I knew as we drove away that she would sneak around to the back of the house and in through the basement door, which she'd left open.

"How'd it go?" asked Charlie as I slid into the car.

Did I smell like spray paint? And cigarette smoke? Fortunately I'd remembered to rub the burnt cork off my face. I rolled down the window.

"Okay," I said.

"Hang in there," he told me.

"A lovely, temperate day ahead," the announcer's voice concluded. It was my clock radio going off on Saturday morning. I'd forgotten to reset it for the weekend. I lay there, feeling generally exhausted and woolly-brained, not thinking about much of anything until the WSTO newscaster segued into the news.

And then I sat bolt upright.

"An old equipment shed at Stoneybrook Middle School burned to the ground last night," she said. "A neighborhood man who saw the fire phoned it in, then rushed to the scene to attempt to contain it. He was badly burned and is now in the local hospital where he is listed in critical condition. Authorities are investigating."

CHAPTER 8

I couldn't believe my ears. I made a lunge for the radio and punched through the stations trying to find another newscast. But radio doesn't have instant replays.

Feeling sick, I sank down on the bed again. It wasn't possible. I was mistaken. I hadn't heard right.

But I knew I had. SMS only had one old shed — the shed that Tonya and Bea and Dilys and I had spray painted last night as our initiation to the SMS softball team.

The fire *must* have started with Tonya and Bea's matches. For a moment I felt a little relieved. A little. Then I remembered the warnings all over the can of spray paint: TOXIC. HIGHLY FLAMMABLE. CONTENTS UNDER PRESSURE.

If a fire had started and come in contact with one of those aerosol cans of paint. . . .

I leaned over and dragged my pack out from

under my bed where I tossed it the night before. The top was half unzipped. I pulled the pack open and pawed through it quickly.

No can of paint.

Had I left the can? Had it fallen out of my pack because I hadn't zipped it up? Had my can of spray paint in combination with Tonya's and Bea's matches caused the fire?

I looked at the clock radio. It seemed like an eternity had passed but it had only been a few minutes. It was still early. But not, I decided, definitely *not* too early to make a few phone calls to three people who should know about the fire.

Late that morning, I let the last person in.

"Hello, Bea," I said. "We're all in my room."

"Is everyone else here?"

"Yeah. Dilys and Tonya are waiting," I said grimly.

Bea didn't seem to be taking the news very hard. She looked around as I led the way to my room and said, "Nice shack, Kristy. Or maybe I should say, shed?"

Then she actually giggled!

"Are you nuts?" I hissed. "Go on!" I pushed her into my room where the other two were waiting and shut the door.

I'd barely gotten it closed before Dilys wailed, "What are we going to *do*?"

"Nothing," said Tonya stonily. "If we don't tell anyone, we probably won't get caught. But if we do get caught, we'll all be in big trouble. And so will the *entire* softball team."

I was stunned. I hadn't thought that far ahead. I'd only thought how terrible it was to have done something like setting a shed on fire — even accidentally — and hurting someone.

Tonya continued, "We're in this together, so we *all* have to keep quiet."

"What about the evidence?" I blurted out. "I mean, we probably left footprints. And cans of spray paint." (I didn't say I left my can of spray paint. That I couldn't find it anywhere.) "Cans that might even have contributed to the fire. And what if that guy who got hurt dies?"

Bea looked suddenly sober. "Dies?" she repeated in a stricken voice.

Tonya shook her head. "He's *not* going to die, okay, Bea? And as for evidence, there've been so many people around that shed just putting out the fire that they'll never find anything.

"The important thing is not to go near the shed, not to say or do anything suspicious, not to even *mention* the fire. We have to stick together."

I'd thought of something else. "What about Tallie and Marcia and the others? They know we were there last night. As soon as they hear the news . . ."

As if in answer to my question, the phone rang. It was Tallie.

"Kristy?"

"Yeah."

"Tallie. You've heard?"

"Yeah. So have Bea and Dilys and Tonya. We're all here."

"Good," said Tallie. "Now listen. If you are caught, even one of you, or if you confess or even breathe one word of this to a living soul, the team will stick together."

For a moment, I thought she meant that the SMS softball team was going to support us. But her next words dispelled that illusion.

"We'll swear there was no hazing, no initiation. That you are lying. That you're making it up so you won't get in trouble for burning that shed down."

"What!" I was outraged. And chilled.

"You'll be on your own," said Tallie. "And you'll be in bigger trouble than ever for lying. You understand?"

"I understand," I said. "Thanks for the — "

But Tallie had already hung up the phone.

"What did she say?" asked Tonya.

"That the team won't back us up if we say the fire got started as part of a hazing. That they'll all swear we're lying to save ourselves."

Bea's eyes were enormous. "Oh, wow," she muttered.

Tonya said, "Then we better not get caught."

"We won't," said Dilys fiercely.

I didn't say anything. I didn't know what to say.

But I felt sick.

CHAPTER 9

Saturday

When you introdused Stacey and me to the Krushers, Kristy, I thought it was prety funny. Like how Karen kept copying everything you did, right down to blowning her own whistel and keeping her own clipbored like yours, and standinng right next to you and doinng everything you did. But now I reelise that if you are coaching, the kids are watching and copying you. For reel. Uh oh!

On Saturday morning, the Krushers and the new coaches had their first practice together. Alone. On the theory that the clothes make the coach (or at least help), Claudia and Stacey had conferred the night before and had dressed up for the occasion. Claudia was wearing a red satin baseball cap, purple sweatpants that were cut off just below the knees, purple high-tops with neon pink laces, red-and-white-striped socks, and a red and pink tie-dyed crop top shirt. Stacey was in black bicycle shorts with neon yellow racing stripes down the sides, a pair of Nikes with matching neon yellow swooshes on the side, (but ordinary white laces), an enormous white v-neck T-shirt, a black jog bra, and a Brooklyn Dodgers baseball cap, turned around backwards. They were both using old gloves of mine. Stacey was wearing my whistle. Claudia had this funky clay whistle shaped like a bird on a leather thong around her neck that she'd made in art class. It didn't really blast like Stacey's, but the Krushers all liked it anyway.

The practice got off to a good start. Stacey looked at Claud, Claud nodded, and Stacey blasted away on her whistle. There was an immediate echo — Karen on *her* whistle — and everybody who hadn't already gathered around the two new coaches came over.

"Good hustle," said Karen approvingly, in exactly the same tones she'd always heard me use.

Suppressing a smile, Stacey said, "Thank you, Karen." She and Claudia looked out over the sea of expectant faces. Then Stacey cleared her throat. "Uh," she began and stopped.

"Why don't you all sit down?" asked Claudia quickly.

"Why?" asked Claire Pike.

"So we can talk about what we're going to do."

"That's after practice," said Karen, consulting her clipboard.

"Today it's before practice," said Claudia firmly. "Everybody sit down."

Everybody sat.

They waited.

Claudia said, "Welcome to Krushers' practice. Today we're going to . . . to . . . practice, uh . . ."

"Softball," supplied Stacey.

"Right," said Claudia.

Linny Papadakis raised his hand and said, "Is this going to take long?"

"No!" said Claudia.

"No," said Stacey. "What we're going to do is divide into two groups and Claudia is going to work with one group and I'm going to work with the other and then at the end of practice the two groups will play a *very* short practice game against each other."

Claire waved her hand in the air and said, "Can I be in Matt's group? He's the best player."

"No fair!" cried David Michael, which was pretty funny, since it is usually Claire who's having a temper tantrum and shouting, "No fair! No fair!" (only it sounds like "Nofe air!").

Sensing that chaos was fast approaching, Claudia gave a blast on her whistle. It wasn't very effective, but the copycat blast that Karen gave right after was — although it also made Claudia jump.

"Uh, thanks, Karen," she gasped. "We're going to divide into groups by counting off. All the ones in my group, all the twos in Stacey's. Karen?"

"ONE!" said Karen in her best outdoor voice.

A little jockeying went on to try to get on the "best" team, but in the end, the two groups seemed pretty evenly divided.

Claudia picked up a ball and her glove and started walking toward the outfield.

"What're we doing?" asked Jamie Newton, eyeing somewhat apprehensively the softball

Claudia was holding (he's afraid of the ball).

"We're going to do a drill," said Claudia brightly.

"What drill?"

"Wait and see," said Claudia.

They reached the outfield. Everyone stopped.

Claudia desperately tried to remember the drill she had in mind. She'd drawn a picture of it when I had shown it to her at the practice the three of us had coached together. She'd filled it in with colored pencils. It had looked pretty terrific.

But what was the drill?

Something to do with junk food. Pop. Soda pop? Pop-tarts?

"Pop ups!" she said at last, triumphantly. It wasn't exactly the drill she remembered, but it was A Drill. And the players were getting restless.

A few minutes later, Claudia was looping balls high (and sort of randomly) in the air and the Krushers were running around underneath, thumping their gloves and trying to catch the fly balls.

It didn't take long for the inevitable to happen: Jamie, running under one of Claud's random high fliers, cringed and then lunged unexpectedly at the last moment. He crashed right into Karen, who said "ooof" and fell down. Karen's glasses went flying.

"Don't move!" screamed Claudia desperately. She had visions of Karen's glasses getting broken and, worse, of someone cutting themselves on the broken pieces (she'd forgotten they were made of safety plastic).

Claudia screamed so loudly that the whole field froze, including Stacey and her team.

Stacey looked over. "Claudia? Is everything okay?"

"Uh, yeah, yeah, here they are . . . everything's fine! No problem. Karen, here are your glasses. Are you and Jamie okay?"

"I'm fine," said Karen, in her most dignified adult manner.

"Me too," said Jamie.

"Shouldn't one of them have called for the ball?" asked Buddy Barrett.

"Called for the ball?" asked Claudia. She had a mystified vision of a fielder calling for the ball and the ball coming, like a dog. But she saw several heads nodding and realized that it couldn't work that way. "Uh, yes," she said firmly. "Next time, call for the ball."

Everyone nodded, satisfied, and went back to practicing catching pop-up fly balls. A few minutes later, the mystery was solved for Claudia when Karen and Hannie Papadakis both ran for a fly ball.

"Mine!" bellowed Karen, and Hannie

stopped while Karen caught the ball.

"Much better!" said Claudia. "See how much better it works when you, ah, call for the ball?"

But the players soon got tired of the fly ball drill and wanted to do something else. In desperation, Claudia suggested sprint races.

"Why?" asked Buddy.

"Because," said Claudia. "It's good for your endurance. Why, on some professional baseball teams, the players run *miles* before they ever even begin a practice." (Was that true? she wondered. Well, it could be. After all, baseball players were athletes, right?)

Claudia ran the players back and forth. Then she made up games, like Keep-Away-From-Being-Tagged-by-the-Player-Holding-the-Ball.

At last it was time for the practice game.

Wearily, Claudia led her team back toward the dugout.

Stacey, she noticed, was looking as weary as Claudia felt. Her Dodgers hat was askew. Her long braid was coming undone. She was covered with smudges.

As for Claudia, one of her socks was all bunched up around the middle of her foot. Her hair kept sticking to her neck. Her hands were sore from catching the ball. And she could barely remember which base came first. Or which base *was* first.

"Who's at bat?" asked Karen.

Claudia looked at Karen blankly.

"Our team'll field first," said Jackie Ro-dowsky. "Since we got to practice in the infield while you guys were in the outfield, you bat first."

"Right," said Claudia weakly.

"What's the batting order?" asked Buddy.

"Batting order?" Claudia had a sudden vision of herself, hands on hips, saying to a player: "I order you to take that bat and hit a home run!"

But that wasn't it.

"You know," Buddy was saying. "The order in which we get to bat."

"Oh. Right," answered Claudia. "Well, uh, Buddy, why don't you go first and, and Karen, you go second . . ." She rattled off four names, concluding with Claire.

"Claire for clean-up hitter?" asked Karen.

Before Claudia could worry about *that*, Claire said mutinously, "Nofe air! I don't want to go last!"

"I'll swap with you, Claire," said Buddy instantly.

That seemed to satisfy everyone, so Claudia agreed.

They only played one inning. It was the

longest inning of Claudia's life. She wasn't sure what a strike was, but she had to be the umpire behind the plate. She heard a half dozen bewildering phrases, including "infield fly rule," "tagging up," and "full count."

And when Jackie Rodowsky slid into home plate he not only managed to uproot the whole plate, but to topple both Matt Braddock, who was playing catcher, and Claudia.

"Watch out!" someone shouted, but it was too late. One minute, Claudia was bent over, hands on her knees, watching the play the way she'd seen umpires on TV do, and the next minute the sky was somersaulting above her head as she fell.

"Safe!" cried Jackie, "I was *safe*. We won, we won!"

Claudia closed her eyes. She hadn't even seen the play.

"It's true," said David Michael. "Matt dropped the ball."

Matt, who is deaf, signed good-naturedly to Jackie, who turned pink with pleasure. "Awesome? Really? Thanks."

Claudia felt them climbing off her. She slowly sat up.

"We won, Claudia," screamed Nina Marshall right in Claudia's ear. "This was great! Wow! I can hardly *wait* till next practice."

It was too much. With a groan, Claudia lay back down next to home plate.

"Claudia?" said Stacey's voice above her. "Claud? Are you okay?"

"It's going to be a long season," Claudia answered and closed her eyes again.

CHAPTER 10

"Burning up the diamond, Kristy?"

The only word I heard was "burning." I must've jumped a mile. My brother Charlie, who was sitting across the dinner table from me, looked surprised.

I managed to laugh. "Sorry. I guess I wasn't listening."

"You weren't eating, either," murmured Nannie.

I realized she was right. I'd been poking at my dinner with my fork.

"You shouldn't play with your food," said David Michael severely.

My whole family laughed at that. I joined in, relieved to be gotten off the hook. Of course I wasn't listening. Or eating. I was worrying. Worrying about the fire. Worrying about the man in the hospital. Worrying about getting caught. And, in a way, almost wishing I would be caught and just get it over.

Only I wasn't off the hook. When the laughter died down (and as I conscientiously began to eat my potatoes, trying to look like I didn't have a worry — or a guilty secret — in the world), Charlie said, "So, how *is* softball going, Kristy?"

"Uh, fine," I said.

"Starting to feel like a team member?" asked Sam.

"Well, that may take some time," I hedged.

"You like Coach Wu?" asked Sam.

"Yes, I do. She really knows how to get her players fired up." I stopped, horrified by my choice of words.

"Speaking of fired up," said my mother, deftly catching a bit of roll that Emily Michelle had sent spinning off her plate, "has anybody heard any more about that fire at SMS? The one that caused the old shed to burn down?"

"No," I said quickly. "Uh, Charlie? I've been meaning to ask you and Sam. Do you think I need to get new softball cleats? Mine are looking kind of worn down, but I don't want to break in new ones right now."

Charlie said, "I'll look at them after dinner. There's some new goop you can put on worn cleats to build them up. Maybe that would work."

"That'd be great."

"It might be better to get new ones now,"

Sam said. "Break 'em in before the season really starts."

"That'd be almost as bad as breaking in a brand new glove right in the beginning of the season," Charlie argued, and they were off and running.

Relieved that I'd been able to divert the conversation, I leaned back. But I couldn't divert my thoughts. I felt horrible. And there was nothing I could do about it.

Except wait. Every time the phone rang, I jumped. Every time someone came to the door, I was sure it was the police, for me. I kept listening to the news, but nothing new was reported about the fire or about the man who had been burned. I wanted to call the hospital and find out how he was, but what if they traced my call? What if someone heard me making the call?

So I waited. I don't even know what I was waiting for. No one was going to give me any good advice. I couldn't tell my friends. And Tallie and Marcia and the others on the team sure weren't going to help.

Even if they did, I thought their kind of help could only make it worse. But then, I didn't see how it was possible for things to get worse.

I was wrong.

When I got to school on Monday, people were talking about the fire. It wasn't the only thing they were talking about, at least not then.

But then Mr. Taylor, the principal, called a special assembly immediately after homeroom that morning. The subject of the assembly was the fire.

Mr. Taylor got up behind the podium, surveyed the room sternly, and cleared his throat. In case any of us hadn't heard the news, he told us, a fire had destroyed the old equipment shed. The man who had reported the fire and helped contain it so it wouldn't spread had been injured and was still in critical condition.

"Of course, the police are investigating the incident," he said. He paused, then went on. "They have gathered enough evidence to suspect that the fire was started by students."

He paused again to let this sink in. A murmur went around the room. Beside me, I heard Mary Anne whisper, "Oh, no! Kristy, do you believe it?"

I kept my eyes fixed on the principal and pretended not to hear.

"I urge the guilty party to step forward," Mr. Taylor said. "I will stay in my office until dinnertime this evening. If anyone wants to come forward, either to tell me why and how he would do something like this — or to give information that would solve this crime — I'll be there. If you do come forward, the matter will be handled as quietly as possible."

This time, I couldn't pretend not to hear Mary Anne. She grabbed my arm and said, "Do you believe it? It can't be true! Who would do something like that?"

"Maybe it was an accident," I said through stiff lips.

"That must be it," agreed Mary Anne as we left the auditorium. "Some kind of accident. Something stored in the shed like paint thinner or something, must have overheated."

"Yeah," I said. "I gotta go, Mary Anne. See you at lunch?"

Mary Anne nodded and waved and turned down the hall toward her first period class. I headed for my locker.

"Kristy!" someone hissed.

I looked up and saw Tonya and Bea standing to one side of the stairwell.

"What do we do now?" said Bea.

"Nothing," Tonya said. "He's just trying to scare us."

I shook my head. "I don't know. But I can't stand it. Why don't we just confess? I mean, who knows what kind of evidence they have — maybe it's *my* can of paint, covered with my fingerprints."

"Forget it," said Tonya scornfully. "And besides, even if they do have that can of paint, it could have been left there anytime. The shed is all burned up, remember? They don't know about the graffiti."

"Have you seen it?" I argued. "Maybe it didn't all burn up."

"Listen, if you tell, we'll say you're lying. And you can't prove we're involved either. It'll be your word against all of ours — the whole softball team. So you'll be in trouble for the fire *and* for lying about us and trying to get all of us in trouble, too!"

With that, Tonya turned and stomped up the stairs. Bea hesitated for a moment longer, then turned and fled after her.

I stood staring after them. I felt sick. I had a horrible lump in my throat and my stomach was hurting and my eyes were blurring.

I stumbled toward my locker and realized as I reached it that the blurring in my eyes was coming from tears threatening to spill over.

Disgusted, I dug my fists into my eyes until I could see.

"Get a grip, Kristy," I muttered to myself. I had to stay calm. I had to think.

But right now the most important thing was to act normal, to get my books from my locker and get to class on time.

I opened my locker and stopped. A square

of white paper had been shoved in through the vents. I picked it up and unfolded it.

And felt even sicker.

In large block letters someone had written:

I SAW WHAT YOU DID. I'M BIDING MY TIME.

CHAPTER 11

Instinctively, I crumpled the note in my hand and looked around. But no one was watching, no one seemed to have noticed my gasp of surprise or my guilty look.

Or at least, no one that I could see.

What should I do now? Who could have written it? What *had* they seen?

Maybe someone else had found my lost can of spray paint.

But then, how would they know it was mine?

The warning bell rang, jerking me back to the present.

I stuffed the note in my pocket, then grabbed my books, and headed for class. But I couldn't focus on anything that was happening.

When I had a chance, I tore the note into tiny little pieces and threw it away — half of it in one trash can and the other half in another. I wasn't taking any chances, although I wasn't exactly sure what chances I wasn't taking by tearing up the note.

I wish I could have thrown my thoughts away, too. *They* weren't so easy to get rid of. Everything seemed to lead back to what I'd done. To someone knowing. To what I could do.

It might have helped if I could have talked to someone, asked someone's advice.

That, of course, was out of the question.

So I went through my classes and through the BSC meeting. Fortunately it was a mondo busy meeting, with practically a phone call a minute, so no one noticed my distraction. Or at least, no one said anything. No one had time to talk about anything else that was happening at school either — like the fire, and how no one had come forward to confess, and who had done it.

The man who had been injured remained in the hospital in critical condition.

By the time Tuesday practice rolled around, I was so tense and uptight that I felt like screaming. The warm weather, the golden sunlight, the velvety green grass that practically screamed, "Play ball!" — none of it helped.

And I wasn't the only one.

We trotted out onto the field like a team.

We did our warm-up laps around the track. We went through the motions of our fielding and hitting drills. From a distance, we probably even looked like a team.

Coach Wu wasn't fooled, though. At first she corrected us patiently, demonstrated over and over the play she had in mind, the pitch or the throw or the batting stance. She tried us in different positions. Nothing helped. We kept on making really stupid mental errors. Finally, as if she realized that all the patience and demonstrations in the world weren't going to help, she went to the third baseline and stood, arms folded, face blank, watching.

That made it even worse.

We began to really make big ME's — mental errors. We turned left when we should have turned right, overthrew the bases on simple plays, swung at the bad pitches, and stood with our bats on our shoulders as the big, fat easy pitches sailed by.

And we began to yell at each other.

When Dilys zinged a ball from third base to first and it flew over Marcia's head, Marcia didn't even try for it. She just threw up her hands in disgust.

"*You* do better!" screamed Dilys. "I'd like to see you."

"With one arm tied behind me!" Marcia screamed back.

"You haven't been doing so hot, Marcia," shouted Tallie unexpectedly.

Marcia's mouth dropped open and we all turned to stare.

That was when Coach Wu stepped in. She blasted her whistle once, then motioned us off the field and into the dugout.

"That's enough for today, team." She looked us all over, measuringly. "Team," she repeated. "Keep that word in mind for the next practice. Dismissed."

She turned and walked away.

No one spoke. Finally, Tallie made a face and headed for the locker room. The rest of the team straggled after her.

In the tense, uncomfortable silence, I changed as fast as I could — and realized that I had forgotten my math book. At least the school was still open and I could get to my locker; one advantage, I guess, to having practice end early.

I raced back to the school and down the quiet halls, grateful that practice was over, that the long day had ended, that I didn't have a BSC meeting or a job that afternoon. All I wanted to do was go home and sit in my room with the door closed, pretending to do my homework. Trying not to think.

Instead, when I yanked my locker open, it was an instant replay in super slo-mo.

Wedged just inside the door was another folded square of paper. I didn't even need to unfold it to know that I would find a note to me in big, square, anonymous block letters. The only difference was, this time, the note was a blackmail note.

I KNOW WHAT YOU DID.
PAY ME FIFTY DOLLARS OR I WILL TELL.

My mouth dropped open.

Fifty dollars? Pay who fifty dollars? And where was I supposed to get *fifty* dollars?

I scooped up my math book, jammed it in my pack and, with the note clutched in one hand, raced back to the girls' locker room. Although it seemed like an eternity since I had hurried down the dark, quiet halls of SMS after practice, it had only been a few minutes. Half the team was still there, getting dressed in gloomy silence.

I skidded around the corner and grabbed Dilys's arm as it emerged from the sweat shirt she was pulling over her head.

"Meet me outside in five minutes!" I ordered.

"Wh-what?" Her head popped through the collar of the shirt. "Oh! Kristy!"

"Five minutes. Outside. Got it?"

"What for?"

"You'll see," I answered grimly. "Tell Bea. I'll get Tonya."

Catching Tonya on the way out the door, I gripped her arm and pulled her to one side.

"Hey! What's this all about?" she protested.

"You'll see." I kept a tight grip on her arm until Bea and Dilys emerged, then motioned all three of them away from the door to the lower corner of the back steps so we could have some privacy.

"Well?" Tonya demanded.

Without answering, I held out the note.

The three of them stared at my outstretched hand for a long moment. Then Tonya took the note and smoothed it out and read it aloud softly.

"Well," she repeated in a different tone of voice.

"Oh," gasped Bea. She began poking around in her gym bag. She pulled out two crumpled pieces of paper — with identical writing and the wording almost the same as mine.

I looked at Bea's note, then I looked at Tonya and at Dilys.

Dilys nodded, then slowly, sheepishly, pulled out three similar notes of her own. And Tonya unfolded a tiny square that she dug up from the corner of her pocket — another note!

104

"We've all gotten them then: threats, demands for money," I said.

"Yeah, well, I don't have that kind of money," said Tonya quickly. She began folding the note back up.

"Neither do I," cried Bea.

"Me, either," said Dilys. "And even if I did . . ." Her voice trailed off.

"What do you want to do?" said Tonya. "It's not like he, or she, left any instructions on how we're supposed to *pay* this money, anyway."

"That's true," I said thoughtfully. "Hmmm. Maybe we should just wait. Whoever is doing it will have to write at least one more note to say how we're supposed to pay this money. If we're observant, and lucky, we might catch him."

Bea said, "I hate this."

"Right, Bea. Like *we* all love it," said Tonya. "Kristy's right. We'll wait. It's all we can do."

Dilys sighed, then nodded. "Yeah."

"Okay, then," I said.

The door to the girls' locker room slammed. We looked up. Tallie and Marcia were standing there. They stared at us and we stared back at them.

I cleared my throat. "See you later," I said loudly to Bea and Tonya and Dilys.

"See ya," murmured Tonya.

As I moved away, I raised my hand and waved at Tallie and Marcia. Tallie gave me a little half wave back. But Marcia just frowned suspiciously.

I gave up. I turned and walked toward the late bus, faster and faster and faster as if I could leave my thoughts and all the terrible things that had happened behind. But of course, I couldn't. Because no matter who had seen what had happened, no matter *who* was blackmailing me, the worst part was that I had brought it on myself. I'd let myself be talked into something I didn't believe in. I'd copied others to try and fit in, instead of being myself.

And now, I didn't like myself very much at all.

CHAPTER 12

Tuesday

Well, it's Stacey (NOT CASEY!) at the bat. And so far, I don't <u>think</u> we've struck out. In fact, you guys would be proud of me and Claud, especially after this last practice on Tuesday afternoon....

"Ah, what a perfect day for softball," said Claudia.

Stacey couldn't help smiling. The weather was nice and, barring any *major* disasters, it probably was a perfect day for softball, which meant, of course, softball practice for the Krushers with Coach Kishi and Coach McGill.

Most of the Krushers had already assembled. As Claudia and Stacey walked onto the field, the team all turned toward them expectantly, exactly, Stacey thought, like those high-speed films of flowers following the sun that she'd seen in biology class.

It was a little daunting to Stacey. But she had experience now, having survived the last Krushers practice. She blew her whistle, clapped her hands, and said, "Hey, everybody, listen up."

Now it was Claud's turn to smile, too.

Stacey looked down at her clipboard and said, "We're going to begin with a little warm-up jog around the field."

Several people groaned. "Hey," said Stacey. "Be cool. This is exactly what Kristy's team at SMS does to start practice."

That got everybody's attention, and in a couple of minutes, she had the satisfaction of seeing the Krushers trotting around the field

— not all together — that would have been too much, considering the age range (and size range) of the team. But all at once, which was good enough.

Stacey was studying her clipboard thoughtfully, where she'd written notes from a basic book of softball, and trying to figure out why she had written the word "fungo" in the margin, when Claudia poked her in the ribs.

"Don't look now, but *look*," Claud hissed.

Coming across the field was Karen. Karen was wearing black bicycle shorts with yellow racing stripes down the side, an enormous white v-neck T-shirt with what looked like a black bathing suit top underneath, a pair of Nikes with white shoelaces, and a hat turned around backwards. If that sounds familiar, it's because it was almost the exact replica of the outfit Stacey had been wearing at the last Krushers' practice, including a baseball hat (plain blue, not the Brooklyn Dodgers one Stacey was wearing) on backwards. With Karen was Ricky Torres.

"Hi!" said Karen brightly.

"Hi, Karen," said Claudia.

"Hey, guys," said Stacey.

In her most grown-up voice, Karen said, "I'd like you to meet Ricky Torres. My *boyfriend*."

Something told Stacey not to say anything like, "What, you mean he's not your pretend husband?"

Claudia said solemnly, "We've met, I believe. How are you doing, Ricky?"

Ricky shrugged. Karen poked him with her elbow. "Uh, fine, thank you," he muttered.

Karen gave Ricky a big, sweet smile and said, "Shall we watch the kids practice?"

"Aren't you going to play, Karen?" asked Stacey.

Karen's eyes got big. "No!" she said, as if Stacey should have known the answer. "Ricky and I are going to watch and . . . and talk to you. You know."

"Oh." The first of the joggers was returning from the warm-up trip around the field. Stacey looked down at her clipboard. "Well, Claud and I are going to be pretty busy . . ."

"That's okay," said Karen. "Ricky and I do not mind. Do we, Ricky?"

Ricky was quicker this time. "Nah," he said.

Claudia was opening the gear bag and pulling out balls and gloves for people to do some throwing drills.

Stacey motioned toward one end of the field. "Walk this way," she said.

Behind her, Claudia immediately began to goof, doing a crazy duck walk. The rest of the team fell in. By the time they reached the outfield, everyone was stifling hysterical laughter and when Stacey looked back, they couldn't hold it in any longer.

Stacey put her hands on her hips and shook her head. Then she started laughing, too.

"How *silly*," said a voice beside her. It was Karen.

"Oh, I don't know, Karen," said Stacey. "I thought it was pretty funny."

"But *childish*," said Karen. "Funny, but childish."

"Mmm." Passing on that one, Stacey went over to Claud and they got the drill organized. It went pretty well, if you ignored the fact that Jackie somehow lost not one but *two* balls.

Karen thought that was "immature." Stacey and Claudia just looked at each other. Karen was trying so hard to be a grown-up. But how could they tell her that being a grown-up didn't mean not having any fun?

The practice meandered along, with Stacey consulting her notes and Claudia improvising and everybody having a good time even if they weren't exactly improving their skills. Ricky got tired of watching after awhile, and soon joined in, but Karen remained stubbornly aloof from the friendly chaos, trying to talk to Stacey and Claudia about nail polish and boyfriends and clothes and magazines whenever she had the chance.

That was when I showed up, after what had been, possibly, the worst afternoon of my entire life, brooding about the horrible practice that had just been cut short, the notes that Dilys, Tonya, Bea, and I had received, everything.

When I realized that getting out of the SMS softball practice meant that I could catch the end of the Krushers' practice, I momentarily forgot my troubles. It was so wonderful to see the Krushers, a team that was one for all and all for one no matter how erratically the individual members played. I watched as Claudia picked up a bat and swung at a pitch thrown by Matt Braddock. She overswung, wrapping herself in a pretzel. Claire and some of the younger kids laughed delightedly and Claudia grinned. As she crouched back down, Matt signed something and his sister interpreted: "Hang in there, Claudia, I mean, coach! You can do it."

It made me laugh while it brought a lump to my throat. I *missed* them.

Just then, Stacey saw me and waved me over. "Kristy. Coach Emeritus!"

"How's it going, Stace?" The sound of Claudia actually connecting with the ball sort of answered the question as I trotted up.

"No problems," said Stacey.

Unfortunately, just at that moment, David Michael, who'd been on first, slid into second base. And slid. And slid. The base had somehow worked loose and sort of skipped off into the outfield when his feet kicked it.

Claudia doubled over laughing at first while Buddy Barrett tagged David Michael triumphantly and shouted, "Yourrrrr OUT!"

"I am NOT," said David Michael. He looked over at Claudia and Stacey. "Am I?"

"Yes," said Stacey.

"No," called Claudia.

"Oh. No," said Stacey, just as Claudia changed her vote to "Yes."

They paused. They looked at each other. Then, by mutual agreement, they looked at me.

"Play it over," I said.

"Uh, Kristy?" said Stacey. "Why don't you take it from here?"

"Well, if you're sure," I said.

Stacey made a neat little bow, and Claudia clasped both hands over her head in a show of support.

I put my hands to my mouth in a megaphone. *"Okay, everybody,"* I shouted. *"Listen up."*

"That is *not* an indoor voice," I heard Karen say disapprovingly.

It wasn't and it felt great. *"Stay where you are,"* I continued. *"We've — you've — got a game against the Bashers coming up, so let's make every minute count!"*

"Yeaaaa, Kristy," Claudia called across the diamond. *"Play ball!"*

CHAPTER 13

"Kristy, over here."

I stopped and looked around. Tonya and Bea were, well, not exactly lurking, but definitely sort of hanging around the front door of the school in a suspicious manner.

Or maybe that was just my guilty conscience that made it seem that way.

"Hi," I said, loudly and (I hoped) not guiltily. I walked over, trying to act casual.

"Have you *heard*?" Bea gasped.

"Heard what?"

"You haven't heard?"

"No, Bea, I haven't heard," I answered, feeling impatient.

"It's great news," Tonya interrupted. "Guess what? It's the boys' baseball team!"

Before I could get Tonya to decode this, Bea explained, "They've been blamed for the fire. The police found the evidence!" She suddenly waved frantically. A moment later, Dilys came up to join us.

As Bea and Tonya repeated the news, I stood there numbly. What a total bomb! I couldn't believe it.

A minute later, I heard Bea say, "And the team has been disbanded. A whole new team is being chosen."

"What?" I heard my voice go up several octaves.

"Kristy. Cool it," said Tonya reprovingly. "Listen, it could have been us. Can you imagine?"

"But they didn't do it, did they?" asked Dilys. She didn't seem as thrilled by the news as Tonya and Bea. But she didn't seem as shocked as I was, either.

Tonya shrugged.

My brain was reeling. The baseball team! It couldn't be! Logan was on the baseball team. Now, because of what we'd done, he wasn't going to get to play this year.

"They couldn't have done it!" I blurted out before Tonya could answer. "What are we going to do?"

"Do?" Tonya looked at me like I was crazy. "*Do?* Nothing. We're off the hook."

"Hooray!" said Bea and she and Tonya gave each other a high-five.

"Except for whoever wrote us those notes," said Dilys softly.

"We can handle that," said Tonya. "After all this, that'll be a piece of cake. Come on, guys." The three of them began to walk away. Tonya looked back. "You coming, Kristy?"

I shook my head.

"See you at practice this afternoon, then."

How could things have gotten worse? Until I'd heard that news, I hadn't believed they could.

Practice that afternoon was a nightmare. But it was only a nightmare for me. Clearly, everyone else on the team had heard the news and clearly they thought it was good news. Tallie and Marcia were laughing and joking and making superstar plays, and teasing Bea and Dilys and Tonya and me good-naturedly. Everyone on the team had the spirit, and if it hadn't been for what I knew, I would have thought it was the best team in the world and I would have been proud to be a part of it.

But I wasn't. And when Coach Wu beamed at us in our post-practice conference and congratulated us on the best practice yet, I didn't feel any cause for celebration.

The BSC meeting was worse.

I arrived to find Mary Anne telling Shannon

all about what had been going on at school in a voice of woe.

"I don't believe it!" Shannon said as I walked in. "The entire baseball team is being disbanded? What kind of proof do they have?"

Mary Anne shook her head miserably. "Logan doesn't know. And he probably won't know until next week. They're going to have a team meeting and the coach is going to talk to them."

"That's terrible, Mary Anne," said Shannon sympathetically.

"Unless they really did it," Claudia put in.

"Logan didn't!" said Mary Anne.

"No!" I heard myself say. "You're absolutely right, Mary Anne."

Mary Anne gave me a grateful look, then said, "Logan says they won't tell them what the evidence is. Everyone's talking, but no one knows anything."

I cleared my throat. "Anyway, this meeting of the BSC will come to order."

If Mary Anne ever found out what I had done to Logan, she'd never speak to me again. . . .

That was the grim start to a grueling weekend. Everywhere I went, everyone seemed to be talking about the vandalism at SMS. Even Karen had heard about it. When I met her and Andrew at the door Friday evening (it was their weekend to be with us) she didn't bound through it as usual. Instead, she clasped her hands in front of her and said, "Can you *believe* it? About the boys' baseball team at your school?"

"Come on in, Karen," I said.

"I lovvve your shirt," said Karen, following me into the house. "Did you get it at the mall? Maybe we could go to the mall tomorrow and shop? Kristy?"

"Maybe," I said absently. "Listen, I gotta go do some homework."

"Do you have a date this weekend?" asked Karen.

"Only with my books," I said as I headed for the refuge of my room.

Behind me, I heard Karen laugh — not a Karen laugh, but a funny sort of breathy, fake-y giggle. "Oooh, Kristy. That is sooo funny."

It went like that all weekend. Mary Anne called and moaned about Logan. Maybe I could help cheer him up, she suggested. Did I want to go to the movies with them?

I thanked her, but said no, she was the best person for the job of cheering Logan up.

Karen tried to talk me into going shopping, then into giving each other a manicure (until I pointed out to her that I didn't wear nail polish *and* that I kept my nails cut short with nail clippers). She followed me around, falling asleep in front of the late night movie I had on Saturday night, after talking about all kinds of weird "grown-up" things and imitating everything I said and did. She even ate exactly what I ate at dinner.

Finally, on Sunday afternoon (after listening to Mom and Watson and Nannie discuss the article in the Stoneybrook paper about the "incident" at SMS all through a late breakfast), I lost it.

Karen had come to my door and knocked.

"Come in," I said, not very welcomingly.

"Kristy, hi!" said Karen, like she hadn't just eaten breakfast with me an hour before.

"Hi, Karen." I looked down at my book pointedly.

"Good book?"

"It's called *Emma*. By Jane Austen. For school."

"Oh." Karen wandered around my room, running her hand over things. Then she saw my sneakers lying on the floor by the closet.

"Oh, Kristy!"

"What?" I said crossly.

"Can I try on your sneakers?"

I lost it. "No! Why? Karen, just leave me alone for five minutes, okay? Five minutes!"

Karen jumped back like I'd hit her.

"But, but Kristy . . ."

"What?" I practically roared, feeling worse than ever and meaner than ever and unable to help myself. "Will you stop following me around? I'm sick of you copying me all the time like some stupid game of Simon Says!"

"I just wanted . . . I mean, but . . . but I want to be just like you, Kristy. That's all . . ."

I opened my big mouth. I closed it again.

"Kristy?" Karen's eyes were enormous.

"Oh, Karen, I'm *sorry*." I felt awful. What could I do? "Listen, I have to tell you something, okay?"

"What?" I could tell that curiosity was overcoming Karen's shock at my yelling at her.

"Don't try so hard to be grown-up."

"But . . ."

"No. Let me finish. I'm flattered that you want to be just like me. But what you should be is just like *you*. If you copy other people, and try to be like other people, it's just, just a big mess."

"A mess?" asked Karen, looking not shocked or curious, but puzzled.

"Trust me, Karen, it's a mess. You're you. No one else is like you in the whole world. So you work on being you, just you, and I'll hang out with you as much as you want. To do it any other way just isn't any fun."

Karen frowned thoughtfully.

"Well," I said gently. "Has it been fun, al-

ways thinking about how you should act to
be like other people?"

"N-no," said Karen. She paused, then said,
"We can still hang out together?"

"Def. Just like always. Give me a little while
and we'll do some major hanging out today.
Okay?"

Karen's expression brightened. "Great.
Super. Gigundoly super!"

"Gigundoly," I echoed as she bounced out
of the room.

After Karen left, I put my head down on
my hands.

Karen had wanted to be just like me.

No, you don't, Karen, I thought. You don't
want to be like me at all. I vandalize things
and burn them down and let other people take
the blame for it.

I hated myself.

And I knew I would go on hating myself
until I did the only thing to do.

I had to confess.

CHAPTER 14

I had to confess, but I had to do something else first. I had to talk to my friends. I cringed at the thought of telling what I'd done, but it was worse not to be able to talk to them about it. And no matter what I'd done, no matter how bad I would look, I knew that they would stand by me.

And if ever I needed the help of my friends, it was now.

I decided to call an emergency meeting of the BSC.

"An emergency meeting? Wow," said Claudia when I called her. "You want to have it here?"

"We can have it at my house," I said.

"Okay," said Claudia. "I'll be there as soon as possible."

"Kristy, is something wrong?" asked Mary Anne when I called *her*.

"Yes," I said. "But I'm hoping you can help."

"Okay," said Mary Anne. And she didn't asked any more questions.

"I'll be there," Shannon told me. "Don't worry."

"Count me in," Stacey said. "Is there anything you need me to do?"

"Just be there and listen," I answered.

In fact, every single member of the BSC was like that. I don't know why I was surprised. I should have known they would be.

When everyone had arrived, I stood up. "This emergency meeting of the BSC will come to order."

Everyone looked at me expectantly. I cleared my throat. *They're not going to stop being your friends*, I told myself. *They're here to help.*

I took a deep breath. Just do it, Kristy, I told myself. "You know that fire at the school? The shed? I'm responsible for it."

"Kristy!" exclaimed Mary Anne. "What are you talking about?"

"I'm talking about my initiation to the SMS softball team. There *are* secret initiations for new members. This year, the initiation was for the new members to spray paint the old shed."

I paused, but no one said anything this time, so I went on. "While we were there, Tonya and Bea started smoking cigarettes. I think

124

that's how the fire started. It was the same night."

For a long moment, the room was silent and I was half afraid to look at anyone.

Then Mary Anne spoke. "What are you going to do?"

"Confess. I can't live with myself, I can't let the boys' baseball team take the blame . . . but first I had to talk to you guys. I shouldn't have done what I did, shouldn't have let myself be pressured into doing something just because everyone else was. It's stupid. Cowardly. I . . . and lying to all of you, keeping this secret . . . that's been awful, too. Because I couldn't talk to you, it was like I didn't have any friends anymore. Like I was all alone."

"You're not alone, Kristy," said Stacey.

"No way," said Claudia.

Jessi and Mallory exchanged glances and then Jessi said, "Count on us."

"Me too," Shannon chimed in.

"What do you want us to do?" asked Mary Anne.

"Don't you want to say anything?" I asked.

"Like what?" asked Claudia.

"Like what I did was wrong. And rotten. And . . ."

"Kristy," Mary Anne interrupted. "You already figured that out. You don't need us to make you feel worse than you do now. And besides, that's not what friends are for."

Stacey rested her hand on her chin thoughtfully, saying, "Plus, it isn't easy to stand up to a crowd. Like when I was trying out to be a cheerleader, remember? We've all gone along with things that we knew weren't right. But now you are trying to do the right thing, and that's what's important."

I swallowed hard. "Oh."

"So," said Stacey with brisk practicality (and maybe because she saw how choked up I was). "What *are* friends for? What can we do in this situation?"

"You're going into the principal's office tomorrow?" asked Mallory.

I nodded, still regaining my self-control.

"You should go in early," said Stacey. "Get it over with. Like a test, you know?"

"Good idea," I managed.

"And we'll go with you," said Mary Anne.

"You will?"

"Yes. We'll be there when you go into his office, and when you come out, okay?"

Everyone else echoed their agreement.

"And even though I can't be there," said Shannon, "I'll be there in my thoughts. Let me know what happens."

"I will," I said.

I surveyed the emergency meeting of the BSC. My friends. How had I gone so long without talking to them? What would I have done without them now?

It didn't bear thinking about.

"Well then," I said, with a slightly watery smile, "this emergency meeting of the BSC is officially adjourned."

That night, I slept well for the first time in a week. I couldn't change what I'd done, but I could do the right thing now. I knew what I was facing tomorrow. I knew I would be facing severe punishment, maybe even being suspended or expelled. But that wasn't so bad as wondering, waiting, feeling guilty and alone.

I wouldn't be allowed to play softball anymore. And even if I were, I wouldn't want to, because I'd be an outcast on my team.

But then, that wasn't my only team. I smiled in the dark, thinking of the Krushers. And I wouldn't be an outcast to my friends.

It was a comforting thought. I turned over and fell deeply asleep and didn't awaken until my clock radio went off.

When it did start, I woke up instantly. For a few seconds, I couldn't recall why I woke up so quickly, and with such a feeling of something huge about to happen.

Then the newscast reminded me. I sat up quickly as the announcer said, " . . . the recent vandalism at Stoneybrook Middle School has been solved."

What! Had someone else — Dilys, Bea, Tonya — confessed?

I leaned closer to the radio, not believing my ears, as the announcer went on, "A group of teenagers from Stoneybrook High School have come forward and confessed to starting the fire that demolished an old shed on the edge of the SMS property. The fire also caused serious injuries to the good samaritan who reported the blaze and attempted to put it out before it got out of hand. The names of the members of the group are being withheld, but one of the members of the group is quoted as saying she couldn't let the SMS baseball team take the blame for something she had done. Another group member, a boy, said, 'My friends and I were looking for excitement, but we didn't mean for anyone to get hurt. We lit the shed on fire and ran away. Then we were going to come back and make a big deal out of putting out the blaze. We thought we would look like heroes, but that guy got out there before we did and anyway, the fire was out of control.' "

I couldn't believe my ears. I was shocked. The fire wasn't my fault after all! I wasn't guilty — or at least, not guilty of arson.

I flung my arms out and fell back in bed, dizzy with relief and amazement and disbelief. Not guilty.

Except of doing what I knew was wrong in the first place. Of being a copycat instead of being myself.

I lay there, being amazed and relieved and feeling wonderful until I heard Nannie's voice calling, "Kristy? Are you getting up this morning?"

"Yes," I shouted, leaping from the bed. I practically danced around the room (although Jessi might not have recognized it as dancing!) and made another amazing discovery: the can of red spray paint wedged under my bed, where I'd slung my backpack the night of the fire. It must've rolled out.

"Aha!" I cried.

"Kristy?" That was Watson.

"Coming," I sang, executing a neat underhand pitch and tossing the spray paint into the garbage.

I wasn't the only one who'd been listening to the news. At SMS, the only topic of conversation on the steps where everyone was hanging out was the fire and the confessions. I saw Mary Anne with Logan as I took the steps two at a time and gave her a thumbs up signal. She smiled and nodded vigorously. I knew the others had heard, too, then. I would see them at lunch and talk it over — quietly and discreetly!

Right now, I needed to see some other people more.

As if my thinking about them had conjured them up, Dilys, Bea, and Tonya emerged from a cluster of people nearby.

"*There* you are," said Tonya. She grabbed my arm and I grabbed Bea's and Bea grabbed Dilys and we all sort of dragged each other off to one side and away from the crowd.

Then we all began to talk at once. We were practically screaming and jumping up and down with relief, possibly even more excitedly than when we'd found out we made the team.

"I don't believe it, I don't believe it!" sang Bea.

"Believe it," said Tonya with a huge grin.

Dilys couldn't stop smiling either, and none of us could stop talking.

"It's over," said Tonya. "It's really over . . ."

Then Dilys said, "Almost."

CHAPTER 15

"Almost!" exclaimed Bea. "What *are* you talking about, Dilys?"

But I knew. We weren't home free. My eyes met Dilys's and by mutual agreement we all began walking further away from the crowd, up the steps and into SMS.

"In here," I said, ducking into the first empty classroom. Students were beginning to mill around outside, going to their lockers, but no one would be so uncool as to head for a class before the first bell.

I pulled the door shut behind us.

"What's going on?" asked Bea.

"We're not home free," Dilys said. "We still did what we did. If that fire hadn't started, people would be talking about who vandalized school property."

Tonya made an impatient sound, but I said, "You're right, Dilys. What we did *was* wrong. But the only thing we *are* responsible for is spray painting the shed. And only the members of the softball team know." (I decided not to mention that the BSC knew, too.)

"So?" said Tonya.

"So it was wrong," said Dilys.

"You don't want to tell anyone?" Bea's voice got shrill.

"I don't know," said Dilys.

"You can't!" exclaimed Tonya.

"I was going to," I said, before Dilys could answer. "I was going to go to the principal's office first thing this morning and confess. Because it was wrong, and because I didn't want the boys' team taking the blame for it."

Bea's mouth dropped open, and Tonya looked surprised. But Dilys didn't.

Dilys said, softly, "Good for you, Kristy. I wish I'd had the nerve to do that."

Tonya started to say something, then stopped. She looked from Dilys to me, and then said, "Well, what good is that going to do now?"

"None," I said slowly. It was true.

"And even if you wanted to fix the shed, to repaint it, you couldn't," Tonya pointed out. "It isn't there anymore."

"Besides, the guy who got hurt is getting better. They say he'll be fine. And the boys' team has been reinstated *and* the principal has offered them a formal apology."

We were all silent, thinking.

Then Dilys said, "I guess there is no need to confess now, after all."

"No," I agreed. "But I don't think there should be any more initiations. Trying out for the team — and making it — is initiation enough."

"How are we going to stop it?" asked Bea.

"We're all members of the team," said Dilys. "We have a vote, too. We *can* stop it."

Another pause and then I said, "So we're all agreed. We don't confess. And we don't do anything *stupid* like this again."

"Agreed," Dilys said.

Bea opened her eyes wide. "Oh, no! What about the notes?"

"The notes. Forget the notes," said Tonya. "No one would believe them, anyway."

"True," I said. "But — "

"I'd still like to know who wrote them," interrupted Bea, which was exactly what I'd been thinking.

Dilys cleared her throat, looking sheepish. "The notes. Well . . . ah . . . I wrote them."

"What!" Tonya jerked around to stare at Dilys, but somehow, now that I'd heard Dilys say it, I wasn't so surprised. She'd always been so quiet, never quite agreeing, never quite disagreeing. But I'd always had the feeling that she'd seen things more as I saw them.

"Yes," Dilys was saying. "Even the ones to myself. I wanted to confess, right from the beginning. I was hoping the notes would force everyone to change their minds."

"I don't believe it," said Tonya. "I don't believe this whole thing. It's unreal."

"It's real, all right," I said. "And I'm never, ever going to forget it. You know what, Dilys? I'm glad you wrote those notes."

"Well, I think all of you are crazy," said Bea. "Me, I'm just glad it's over. Really over. Now we can play ball!"

The first bell rang just then, and the thunder of people heading into the building to class began to build in the halls.

"See you at practice," I said.

We left the classroom and went our separate ways. The day was just beginning, but I already felt like I'd lived through a lifetime. I wasn't complaining, though. Just then, life felt great.

"Are you still going to play on the team?" Mary Anne asked me at lunch.

"Maybe. I don't know," I said. "Some things will have to change . . ." I stared down at my lunch and gave something gray and squishy a tentative poke. "You know what? This isn't lunch. It's compost."

"Kristy!" wailed Mary Anne.

"Some things will *never* change," said Stacey.

We all began to laugh. It felt like forever since I'd been able to laugh with my friends. And it felt great.

I was thinking about that moment as I got ready for practice that afternoon. Me and my friends, laughing together.

Maybe I could work things out with my team. Learn to play with them, teach them a few things, too. The first game was coming up, and I wanted to play in it. I liked some of my teammates, like Dilys, especially. Coach Wu was terrific.

Being on the team could be terrific, too.

I decided I'd wait and see. But whatever happened, I was never, ever going to give in to pressure again and do something that made me feel uncomfortable. I was going to stand up for what I believed in. Because as corny as it was, it was true: it wasn't just whether you won or lost.

It *was* how you played the game.

About the Author

ANN M. MARTIN did *a lot* of baby-sitting when she was growing up in Princeton, New Jersey. She is a former editor of books for children, and was graduated from Smith College.

Ms. Martin lives in New York City with her cats, Mouse and Rosie. She likes ice cream and *I Love Lucy*; and she hates to cook.

Ann Martin's Apple Paperbacks include *Yours Turly, Shirley; Ten Kids, No Pets; With You and Without You; Bummer Summer;* and all the other books in the Baby-sitters Club series.

Look for BSC #75

JESSI'S HORRIBLE PRANK

Kids were zooming back and forth. A girl carrying light bulbs almost collided with a guy carrying props. Ben was practicing the steps for the finale. Three girls were singing the words, to help him out.

It was an absolute, total zoo.

"How do ah look?" Jamie said, standing up in her full Dolly getup.

"Beautiful," I replied. "And me?"

"Well . . ."

We looked soooo stupid. It was hilarious.

The hallway clock said 7:35. Twenty-five minutes to go. I had to see the audience.

The Pikes were negotiating their seats, making a whole row of people move over. Kristy and her family were sitting right behind them. Claudia was in the back of the auditorium, gabbing with Mary Anne and Logan.

So many people were filing in. The auditorium was almost half full. In just a little while the lights would dim, and we'd be on our way.

I started to shiver. The Follies were nothing like a ballet performance. No routines, no music to guide me along. Just me, Jamie, and the audience. If we did well, they'd laugh. If not . . . well, I didn't want to think about that.

"Pssssst! Jessi!"

I looked down at the front row. Becca was waving to me, grinning from ear to ear. I could tell Mama was trying not to screech with laughter at my outfit.

Daddy didn't see me. He was helping Aunt Cecelia with her coat. She, of course, looked exasperated.

Then, out of the corner of my eye, I saw *him*.

Mr. Trout.

He was walking into the auditorium, alone. His toupee was shiny in the glare of the house lights. He took a seat way in the back, opened up a paperback, and started reading.

Suddenly my stomach felt like a pinball machine. I let the curtain fall in front of me.

All my doubts came rushing back into my brain.

What was I doing?

Mysteries:

4 *Kristy and the Missing Child*
Kristy organizes a search party to help the police find a missing child.

5 *Mary Anne and the Secret in the Attic*
Mary Anne discovers a secret about her past and now she's afraid of the future!

6 *The Mystery at Claudia's House*
Claudia's room has been ransacked! Can the Baby-sitters track down whodunit?

7 *Dawn and the Disappearing Dogs*
Someone's been stealing dogs all over Stoney-brook!

8 *Jessi and the Jewel Thieves*
Jessi and her friend Quint are busy tailing two jewel thieves all over the Big Apple!

9 *Kristy and the Haunted Mansion*
Kristy and the Krashers are spending the night in a spooky old house!

#10 *Stacey and the Mystery Money*
Who would give Stacey counterfeit money?

#11 *Claudia and the Mystery at the Museum*
Burglaries, forgeries . . . something crooked is going on at the new museum in Stoneybrook!

#12 *Dawn and the Surfer Ghost*
When a local surfer mysteriously disappears, Dawn fears his ghost is haunting the beach.

#13 *Mary Anne and the Library Mystery*
There's a Readathon going on and someone's setting fires in the Stoneybrook library!

THE BABY-SITTERS CLUB®

by Ann M. Martin

More titles... ▶

The Baby-sitters Club titles continued...

☐ MG45659-8	#58 Stacey's Choice	$3.50
☐ MG45660-1	#59 Mallory Hates Boys (and Gym)	$3.50
☐ MG45662-8	#60 Mary Anne's Makeover	$3.50
☐ MG45663-6	#61 Jessi's and the Awful Secret	$3.50
☐ MG45664-4	#62 Kristy and the Worst Kid Ever	$3.50
☐ MG45665-2	#63 Claudia's *Freind* Friend	$3.50
☐ MG45666-0	#64 Dawn's Family Feud	$3.50
☐ MG45667-9	#65 Stacey's Big Crush	$3.50
☐ MG47004-3	#66 Maid Mary Anne	$3.50
☐ MG47005-1	#67 Dawn's Big Move	$3.50
☐ MG47006-X	#68 Jessi and the Bad Baby-Sitter	$3.50
☐ MG47007-8	#69 Get Well Soon, Mallory!	$3.50
☐ MG47008-6	#70 Stacey and the Cheerleaders	$3.50
☐ MG47009-4	#71 Claudia and the Perfect Boy	$3.50
☐ MG47010-8	#72 Dawn and the We Love Kids Club	$3.50
☐ MG45575-3	Logan's Story Special Edition Readers' Request	$3.25
☐ MG47118-X	Logan Bruno, Boy Baby-sitter Special Edition Readers' Request	$3.50
☐ MG44240-6	Baby-sitters on Board! Super Special #1	$3.95
☐ MG44239-2	Baby-sitters' Summer Vacation Super Special #2	$3.95
☐ MG43973-1	Baby-sitters' Winter Vacation Super Special #3	$3.95
☐ MG42493-9	Baby-sitters' Island Adventure Super Special #4	$3.95
☐ MG43575-2	California Girls! Super Special #5	$3.95
☐ MG43576-0	New York, New York! Super Special #6	$3.95
☐ MG44963-X	Snowbound Super Special #7	$3.95
☐ MG44962-X	Baby-sitters at Shadow Lake Super Special #8	$3.95
☐ MG45661-X	Starring the Baby-sitters Club Super Special #9	$3.95
☐ MG45674-1	Sea City, Here We Come! Super Special #10	$3.95

Available wherever you buy books...or use this order form.

Scholastic Inc., P.O. Box 7502, 2931 E. McCarty Street, Jefferson City, MO 65102

Please send me the books I have checked above. I am enclosing $_____
(please add $2.00 to cover shipping and handling). Send check or money order - no
cash or C.O.D.s please.

Name _____ Birthdate_____

Address _____

City_____ State/Zip _____

Please allow four to six weeks for delivery. Offer good in the U.S. only. Sorry, mail orders are not
available to residents of Canada. Prices subject to change.

Create Your Own Mystery Stories!

MYSTERY GAME!

WHO: Boyfriend   **WHY:** Romance

WHAT: Phone Call   **WHERE:** Dance

Use the special Mystery Case card to pick WHO did it, WHAT was involved, WHY it happened and WHERE it happened. Then dial secret words on your Mystery Wheels to add to the story! Travel around the special Stoneybrook map gameboard to uncover your friends' secret word clues! Finish four baby-sitting jobs and find out all the words to win. Then have everyone join in to tell the story!

Now THE BABY-SITTERS CLUB®

★ is a Video Club too!